INTO THE MOORS

THE
BRIDGE
BETWEEN
WORLDS

MK SHEVLIN

Dedication

For
Gina

The bestest sister ever.
The bestest human ever.
The kindest soul I know.

I love you Beanz…

Table of Contents

Table of Contents

foreword

Whilst this book is categorised as a fantasy novel in bookstores and online, who's to say it isn't actually a true, historical document or perhaps, even an autobiography of sorts?

Who's to say these events didn't actually happen long ago, here and possibly in another reality? That these characters weren't real, and their journeys not shared by sentient trees with those who have open hearts and minds to listen?

Not me... don't you know...

MK Shevlin

Prologue

The Prophecy

ÚTÍRADIEL HAD LONG been expected to be the new augur of the Aoileach people. Her mother, grandmother, and great-grandmother had all served as seers in Caledonia for as far back as anyone could remember. Útíradiel certainly had the gift of sight from very early in her childhood. She had often seen things that no one else could, even if only briefly. The visions came unbidden, several times a day. Some were clear, like waking dreams, whilst others were fragmented and scattered like smoke rings dissipating in the air. All possessed a strange certainty that caused her to recognise their truth despite their elusiveness.

Útíradiel was an even odder child than her mother Valainistima had been. She would often be found walking along the riverbed, collecting her own special set of Rune-Rocks. Occasionally she would be seen casting spells and setting the river alight, to compel it to give up its secrets. Her white left eye, which had clouded her vision from the time she was seven, frightened other children and kept them distant. Her odd personality destined her to be alone and nearly friendless. She was appointed augur just prior to her own mother's death, two days before Útíradiel's fifty-ninth birthday.

Her words were always wrapped in poetic riddles, often without context, making it difficult for the Aoileach to comprehend. Even when she answered a simple question, there were so many layers in her words it was as if she had said nothing at all.

Many of the elders were concerned about this strange woman becoming their spiritual leader. Edmund's brother, Tad, believed the elders should welcome her without question. After all, no one could deny that Útíradiel had the sight, and with the darkening shadows to the east, the growing number of battles between the Firbolgs and Tuatha, and so many sightings of Black Harbingers throughout the forest, she seemed to be their only hope.

The Firbolgs, a race of fierce warriors with skin like tree bark and the Tuatha De Danann, a tribe of ginger-bearded barbarians, had been growing in number and power. Their hatred of each other went back hundreds of years, when both races nearly destroyed each other over a woman. Dark rumours still lingered about their bloodstained battles that had taken place long ago, whispered stories of death and destruction so terrible that they could only be legend. But now skirmishes between them and the deaths of all who stood in their way made the legends reality.

Then came *the Wasting*. A horrible disease that was spreading throughout the land like wildfire, sweeping across the continents and leaving nothing but death in its wake. The men affected by it wasted away slowly, first losing their minds, and then their strength was sapped until they were nothing but paper-thin skin and bone. The women who had borne children were also susceptible, though their demise from the Wasting was even more horrific. Their abdomens would swell, becoming hard and grey in colour. They would eventually explode, the flying dust spreading the Wasting to any and all who were nearby. Panic spread as fear gripped everyone.

Valainistima's final vision before her death was one of war with the Firbolgs and Tuatha, who would become known as the Guundalin, perhaps only a few years away, but between the war and the Wasting, their way of life would end. Útíradiel was directed by the elders to use her sight in hope of finding redemption for her people as the dark hour approached.

Útíradiel sat in the ashes of the now-cold community firepit. In her lap, she held a shallow, elongated bowl made of melted rock. It was rimmed with quartz, amethyst, and clear crystal. Her long, pale ginger hair, streaked in white, hung down, obscuring her face as she mumbled repetitive chants learned from her mother. She lit a stick of sage incense, its smoke swirling around her like red ribbons. She sprinkled a strange-smelling yellow powder on the surface of the stones within the bowl.

Several of the rocks glowed red. She carefully stirred some away and discarded them into the ash at the bottom of the firepit.

The auger seemed to enter a trancelike state as the elders, including Tad and Edmund, watched from a nearby fallen tree trunk now being used as a bench.

The vision unfolded in Útíradiel's mind:

Onawah gently caressed her very pregnant belly. Her dress was stretched tightly against it. Only a few more days, the medicine woman told her, and it would be over. Her husband, Bear Head, had demanded she give him a son, but to Onawah, the unborn child felt and moved more like a girl. She feared Bear Head would be angry with her, but in her heart, she indeed hoped for a daughter. She had already chosen a name, Miramanee. It wasn't a tribal name, but she liked the sound of it on her tongue.

The relocation to Sand Creek had been difficult for her and the two tribes, the Cheyenne and Arapaho. Winter had settled over them early and hard on these barren plains. A coat of dirty, sand-filled snow, driven by the icy winds, blanketed the landscape in patches. Their tribal leaders, Black Kettle and Left Hand, had chosen relocation rather than war. Onawah didn't care for the white men or their stern faces and odd ways, especially that Colonel Chivington. He always seemed angry, and his eyes were too close together for her liking, but she trusted her husband.

Onawah bundled up in her coarse, thick buffalo skin and left the warmth of her teepee to relieve herself near the stream. During the summer, this stream was dry, but now, with the heavy snow and occasionally warmer days, it ran strong and cold. She also felt the brisk walk would do her well, as she had rarely left her lodge over the past few weeks due to the snow and bitter cold. The air was clean and smelled lightly of smoke from fires that were tended by diligent women for their families. Her breath frosted into tiny crystals that lingered in the air. She smiled and watched the young boys attempting to play a game of hoop and pole, though the hoop wasn't cooperating in the deep ruts of the packed snow. As they tried to roll it forward on the ground, it often flopped over onto its side or toppled into a drift before the pole throwers had even a moment to try to toss the pole through the small, nearly invisible opening in the hoop.

As Onawah reached the edge of the stream and squatted to relieve herself, she noticed soldiers approaching her settlement on horseback. As the tribal leaders went out to greet them, they began screaming and charging her people. She could hear gunfire and watched the Cheyenne and Arapaho braves falling and being trampled under the soldiers' horses. Onawah froze in terror, unable to even breathe. The soldiers began torching the lodges and slaughtering the women and children as well. Onawah vomited onto the ground as she witnessed two soldiers cut open the womb of another pregnant woman and then dismember her and her child.

Onawah had to hide or the soldiers would do the same to her, but where? She scanned her surroundings—the soldiers had not seen her yet, but it was only a matter of seconds before they would.

Crawling on all fours, Onawah moved toward the hillside ridge nearest her. She could hide there. She began moving upstream, staying low and close to the snow-banked edge. She tried to move as silently as possible, but it was too late. Two of them had spotted her and her bright yellow leggings, about an eighth of a mile upstream.

Onawah's lead was no match for their horses. They were gaining on her fast. As the snow slowed her progress, Onawah jumped into the freezing water in hopes of escape.

She stumbled over the slippery rocks in her long leather leggings, nearly falling over with each desperate step.

Onawah could hear the sound of the horses' hoofs and soldiers approaching, but she didn't look back. She was nearly around the protruding earth and rocks, and in a moment she would be on dry land and could make a run for it.

The sound of a single gunshot reverberated through the crisp winter air. Onawah heard a faint whizzing sound but, before she could even react, she felt a searing pain in the back of her knee. The bullet passed clean through, shattering her kneecap and spat it out the front of her leg. Everything seemed to happen in slow motion to Onawah, but the overwhelming agony was instantaneous. She tumbled face-first into the water.

A brief moment of stunned silence followed as Onawah raised herself onto her elbows. She knew what was coming next: her death and that of her daughter, Miramanee.

Strength of will took hold of Onawah; she was determined to fight for her life and that of her daughter. She dragged herself onto dry ground, hoping to find a place to hide. Her spirit sank as there was nothing but a series of solid rocks embedded into the edge of the low hillside with empty, endless grasslands beyond. There was nowhere to hide. She decided if this was to be the end, she would face it as the wife of a great warrior.

The horses were nearly upon her. Onawah dragged herself over to the vertically straightest part of the rock protruding from the hill. It was a place she could face her murderers. She would show them no fear.

The rock, embedded into the hillside, was nearly six feet tall. As she pulled herself up into a standing position, Onawah blinked back tears and uttered no sound from her lips despite the excruciating pain she felt.

The horses were only seconds away. Onawah and her daughter would soon join her husband and fellow tribesmen in the afterlife. She leaned back onto the large grey rock for support and to face her enemies. She dug her fingers into the rough surface and braced herself, but the rock gave way to nothingness, and Onawah felt herself falling backward into shadow. The world spun in dizzying circles around her, and then darkness.

Onawah opened her eyes. She was surrounded by a thick forest. Trees towered above her like ancient sentinels, their bark gnarled and knotted with age in the dense fog. Each tree was laden with varying shades of grey. The air was thick and unyielding—like trying to inhale soup. She gasped. Only after a moment with it in her lungs did it feel like air. She almost felt like she was choking on it. Was this the afterlife? Surely not, she thought to herself as she looked all about.

Eerie light filtered through the silent, motionless trees above her, like sparkling diamonds, casting dappled shadows across everything beneath it. Onawah noticed that some of the leaves appeared to be made of glass or crystal, glinting in the light.

She turned her head to the other side. To her surprise, a small creature resembling a tiny woman with white wings was suspended in the air before her. She studied Onawah with great curiosity. She was only about seven or eight inches tall and seemed to be moving very slowly. Her face was difficult to make out in the grey light, but she was quite pretty and had a gentle face. Was this a spirit sent to greet her? Her big, round eyes were inquisitive, and she looked as innocent as a child. Onawah reached out with one hand, but she was too far away to touch the spirit. She tried to speak; no words came. The tiny woman spoke, but Onawah's ears could not hear her. She seemed to be asking her questions, but Onawah could not answer. The pain in her leg was excruciating. Onawah's lifeblood was draining from her body. As darkness began enveloping her, she spotted something moving behind the strange little creature. Something large, something dark, something moving lightning fast. Three tall creatures now stood above her. They resembled skeletons wrapped in wet gauze. They looked down upon her with their hollow eye sockets. Onawah screamed in terror as all went dark.

Onawah's eyes flickered open to the sensation of soft linens against her skin. Confusion and fear grasped her heart as she saw several women surrounding her. Their ears were pointed, and they were wearing strange clothing. She frantically searched her belly, feeling a flatness that had not been there for many months.

"My baby! My baby!" she *cried out in her native tongue, her voice quivering with desperation.*

A pair of gentle hands rested on Onawah's shoulders, anchoring her to this new reality. One of the odd-looking women sat down next to her on the bed, softly taking her hand in hers. Her voice was comforting, though Onawah couldn't understand her words. Another woman approached the bed, holding something wrapped in a soft blanket, and presented it to Onawah.

The wrappings were softer than any woven fabric Onawah had ever felt, almost like clouds beneath her fingertips. As she opened the blanket slightly to reveal her newborn daughter, she saw cherubic cheeks and tiny fingers grasping at the surrounding air. The child's cry sounded like music to Onawah's ears; much like the first whispers of spring bringing forth new life after a cold winter. She openly wept tears of joy. As she freed one of her breasts to feed the hungry girl, Onawah smiled and thanked the women the best she could.

"Miramanee. Her name is Miramanee!" Onawah *proudly proclaimed.*

The augur's milky-white eyes opened wide, having seen through the veil of time itself. The vision had ended, but its impact lingered on her face, which was etched with a look of profound understanding. With this vision, she knew the salvation of the Aoileach.

The Imrami gathered around her, anxiously awaiting her words like children waiting for a bedtime story. Edmund stood beside them, almost vibrating with anticipation; he had longed to hear the words of the seer since becoming an elder.

Tad couldn't help but notice how his brother was fidgeting with excitement and remembered when he'd felt the same way during his first hearing of the augur's prophecy. Tad smiled with fondness at the memory as he stroked his coal-black beard.

The whole group fell silent as the augur prepared to speak, her voice carrying an otherworldly quality that commanded attention and respect.

"Salvation's womb is among us, and what it spits shall be among us again when the time is near. Two daughters, one yet to be… On the third harvest, the daughter of both worlds will be birthed: the daughter of … Edmund Turly and Miramanee. She will be *the Bridge between Both Worlds*. This daughter of both worlds will be the protector-mother. In her seventh year, she will be exiled into the otherworld until her thirty-forth year."

Edmund froze at the augur's words. He was going to marry the outsider, the Indian woman's daughter? They would have a child together and then exile the child?

Tad looked over his long beak nose at Edmund with a smile. "So much for being a single man, eh, Edmund?"

Edmund sat speechless.

The augur continued. "The Hidden Child, born of Mer and Elf, fair and frail, brought to us a fortnight past. The Hidden Child, born of Mer and Elf, fair but frail, though not of us. The Hidden Child—the Unloved Child—will return the light of life to Caledonia and Balynfirth from the bitter world. The Hidden called *Minastauriel.* The daughter of both worlds will bridge the path home for herself and the return of the Hidden. The Hidden Child, born of Mer and Elf, frail and fair. The Unloved Child's lifeblood will end the *Wasting,* but be warned. She brings the Daemose. The two heads will become one. Daemose will be loosed. The Hidden Child... must be hidden."

Chapter One

The Cabin

I T WAS LATE April, though none of the girls knew the exact date. A thick layer of snow masked the moorland landscape in white, like a blank canvas for the wind to paint upon. Dark green shoots of grass and heather poked up through the canvas, teasing that spring was beneath it, soon to be revealed.

The girls shivered in the freezing temperatures, biting winds, and what seemed to be a permanently overcast sky. Their breath froze before them, only to dance away into nothingness. Theresa encouraged them to be grateful for the harsh conditions; their food would last longer, the ground was firm to walk on, and they would be able to travel more quickly.

Katie fussed openly for several hours, even as her lips became so numb her speech was now slurred, making her thick accent much worse, and though no one could understand a single word she spoke, on she rambled.

Hilary stayed close to Mina, their arms locked together in silence as they trudged through the snow.

Mina held a piece of wolf fur over her ear as they walked. When her arm grew tired, Hilary would take over ear-guard duty, trying her best to keep the bitter winds away.

Theresa guessed Mina was in great pain and infection was setting in. Suddenly something caught her eye in the distance. She strained to see what was appearing and disappearing every few seconds before them as the blowing snow revealed and then concealed it like a cruel game. Like a snow globe gone mad.

"Now you see it. Now you don't. Now you see it. Now you don't!" Katie quipped.

The swirling winds subsided for a moment, and the blowing snow crashed to the ground, revealing what lay before them: a log cabin.

Theresa turned her eyes to the shivering Mina. Snowflakes had melted beneath her frosted eyelashes, then run down her cheeks and frozen into place.

"Is this the cabin, the cabin in your dream?"

Mina nodded, lowering her eyes to the ground, and Theresa quickly wrapped her arms around the girl, trying to comfort her as she looked around frantically. There was no other option. Darkness was descending, and they had to shelter immediately.

Theresa looked deep into Mina's eyes, eyes filled with such fear. "We have no choice."

The aged building appeared to have been abandoned for many years, perhaps many decades. Its frame, though somewhat crooked, was well constructed. Instead of nails, wooden wedges held each nearly petrified log firmly in place. The small single window of the cabin had no glass but was sealed tightly, a hinged slat of wood covering it firmly and locking from within. Even the roof was made from split logs on a sharp slope so as not to gather water or snow. A heavy peat thatch had once covered the roof, though much of it had eroded away, exposing the wooden logs.

Strangely, the cabin seemed to be built right into the rocky hillside. Theresa felt the seam where the logs blended into the rocks.

"How odd," she said to herself.

The stiff winds had deposited snow knee-deep at the doorway, and she kicked it away from the wooden door as the girls huddled closely together, shivering in anticipation of shelter. She banged on the door loudly.

"Hello? Anyone here? We need help! Hello?"

The door was hinged with leather straps, and the settling of the building had wedged it in tightly; it wouldn't budge. There was no handle but rather a small rectangle cut out of the wood that she was able to grasp and unlatch. She pushed the door inward. A thin flap of leather inside the opening was nailed at the top to keep the weather and insects out.

Theresa struggled against the door but could only free the very bottom of it. The top was welded tightly against the settled doorframe.

"Katie!" Theresa commanded. "Give me a hand!"

Katie quickly came to Theresa's aid. Soon the bottom two-thirds of the door was moving.

Mina seemed confused and looked poorly. Hilary squeezed her hand and smiled. "It'll be okay." Then she left Mina's side to help free the door.

Mina now stood alone, shivering violently. After a long moment, the top of the door splintered off and suddenly swung inward, startling her.

Katie moved to enter the shelter, but Theresa grasped her shoulder. "Wait!" she commanded with an index finger pointed firmly at Katie. With that, Theresa slowly entered the dark cabin. Pulling her lighter from her pocket, she lit it. *Flick, flick!*

"Hello? Anybody... home?" Theresa said in almost a whisper.

"I reckon iz only ghosts living here now, T'reeza," Katie called out from the doorway.

Dim light filled the room, and Theresa cautiously eyed the strangely familiar surroundings. The ceiling beams were low and exposed, and the room was blanketed with dust and cobwebs, all stirred up by their arrival. The air was thick with the smell of damp earth and rotting wood. At the far end of the cabin was an old oak table with benches on either side. Six large candles in the centre surrounded a bowl filled with what looked like rocks from the riverbed. She ran her finger around the rim of the wide bowl and the stones. They seemed very familiar.

Near a stone wall was an old rocking chair—the only sign of life in this forgotten place—that seemed to yearn for company after so many years alone in the empty moors.

She cautiously scanned the room one more time, then blew the dust from the candles and lit them. Light quickly filled the room, revealing its secrets.

She ushered the girls in out of the cold and, with Katie's help, repositioned the door in its proper place, leaving the frigid darkness on the doorstep.

A small cast-iron stove stood in the corner. Nearby, a large tin of coal and a rusted old spade plunged deep into the black rocks with a box of long matches. Hilary inspected the stove, dusted it off, and within minutes had heat radiating from it.

Theresa noticed Mina crouched in a corner, holding her hand to her ear, and squatted down next to her. Theresa's own lips were still numb from the icy winds. "Your ear?"

Mina nodded, a sad pout covering her face.

"I'm sorry, Mina. Hopefully it won't hurt as much once you've warmed up. Let's move closer to the stove."

Mina nodded again and took Theresa's outstretched hand.

Theresa led Mina to the stove, then lit one of the oil lamps on a shelf. Katie joined in the exploration of the small cabin whilst Hilary took to dusting off the table with an old linen she had found.

After a moment, Katie called out cheerfully, "Iz all right, this! A bit of paint. Some wallpaper. A wolf rug or three on the floor. This place will be sweet!"

Long rows of shelves were filled with canning jars. Katie began rubbing the sooty dust from the handwritten labels: TOMATOES, CARROTS, GHERKINS, POLE BEANS, COURGETTES, and POTATOES.

On the shelf below were two sacks of some type of grain or perhaps beans. Next to the sacks stood several jugs containing a brownish liquid, a rack of dusty wine and mead bottles, and several large cooking pots and wooden utensils.

"You fink iz still good?" Katie asked in eager anticipation.

Theresa paused for a moment to think. "Grab two of each except the gherkins, yeah? I'll check the seals."

"You don't fancy gherkin soup, eh?" Katie said with a sly grin and a wink.

Theresa smiled at Katie. "We might be having a proper stew for dinner tonight, Miss Katie!"

Katie's eyes lit up. "Roight!"

Theresa carefully inspected each of the jar's seals for decay and rust. All the containers but one looked, smelled, and tasted fine. She set Katie to gather a cooking pot, utensils, and hopefully a paring knife and some spice.

"I cannae find spices or fohks!" Katie said, rummaging through a box under the shelves.

"Check in the second drawer and cupboard just above the jug of Scottish ale, Katie. They should be in there," Theresa replied without thinking as she continued draining off the liquid from the vegetables and filling the large pot.

Suddenly she stopped, realising what she had just said, and turned toward Katie, whose eyes were fixed on her.

Holding up a handful of forks, spoons, and several containers of spices, Katie eyed Theresa suspiciously. "'ow did you know that?"

Theresa froze. "I... I don't know..." The sense of familiarity with this place suddenly overwhelmed her. She stood silent for a moment, studying the pantry shelves. "The jug on the left is Scottish ale... the one on the right is stout."

She slowly walked over to where the jars of carrots resided, dug into her pocket, and pulled out her pipe. After looking at it for a moment, she reached up to the highest shelf and, standing on her toes, retrieved a pouch that was hidden from view.

Theresa wiped the dust from the label. RED STEM LEAF. She stared at it for a moment. "What's going on here?"

"How did you know?" Katie asked.

Theresa stood silent. Memory flashes flooded her mind.

"Wait... This place is called the Wait. We... we had to stay here for a week or two... Time. Something about time. We had to catch up with time. We had to wait here until time... Tad... Tad kept the tobacco on the top shelf... to keep me out of it. He said I was too young."

Theresa's eyes followed the shelves to the end. She then made her way towards a dark corner and pulled something from the shadows— an old rifle with cobwebs woven all about it and an empty chamber. The sound of a shot echoed in her mind as she remembered what had happened here; this wasn't just a cabin...

After a moment, she loaded her pipe with the red stem leaf and sat down in the rocking chair, lost in thought and smoke rings.

Hilary took over the dinner preparation and finished placing the tomatoes, potatoes, carrots, and beans in the pot. Mina joined her when Hilary's face expressed confusion as to what the next step was.

"I wish Kat was here. She'd know how to do this proper," Hilary mumbled aloud.

"Kat's resting now," Mina replied.

"How did you know?" Hilary said with wide eyes.

"Gather a bit of *white* snow—don't use *yellow* snow; it doesn't taste very good—and put it in with the vegetables. When you cook it, the snow will magically turn into broth, don't you know," Mina said.

Hilary complied and set the pot on the metal stove. It sizzled as the melting snow on the outside of the pot met the red-hot metal.

Shortly the pot of stew began to bubble. Theresa spiced it and, to everyone's displeasure, put the rest of the wolf meat into the pot after dicing it into bite-sized pieces. The girls let out a collective moan at the sight.

"Sorry, girls. We need to use it up before it goes off. With all the spice I've put into it, it will taste just like a proper beef stew. So no fussing!"

Katie, looking disgusted, let out a loud sigh. "Roight."

With a raised eyebrow, Theresa gave her a warning glance. Understanding the look, Katie comically dropped her head onto the hardwood table with a *thud*.

Hilary giggled under her breath at the sight, only to catch Theresa's eyes now on her. She gulped.

"The Eye of Theresa is upon you, Hilary!" Katie said melodramatically. "Muahaahaahaa! Muahaahaahaa!"

Theresa couldn't help but smile. She had forgotten what it was like to have children around, the playfulness, the laughter, and the innocent humour.

As the stew simmered, Theresa returned to the rocking chair and stared at the rock wall at the far end of the cabin. Something about that wall had her mesmerised. Something she couldn't quite remember…

"Dinner is served!" Hilary announced cheerfully. To Theresa's surprise, Hilary had set the large wooden table with a place for each of them. The meal, in spite of the wolf meat, was filling and, best of all, hot.

With a warm cabin and a hot meal, everyone seemed in much better spirits. Conversation and laughter broke out as the respite from the previous days applied a healing poultice to the physical and emotional wounds each had suffered.

"In the morning," Theresa said, "we are heading to a village not far from here. I'm going to ring Miss Medlock and arrange transportation for all of us and try to find a proper doctor to attend to Mina's ear. It will be several days, I'm sure, before anyone can come for us, so we will be staying there until then."

"Why cannae we stay here?" Katie interrupted. "This could be our new home... for ole of us!"

"Katie," Theresa replied, "this isn't our home. My home, my life, is a long way from here. You and Hilary were entrusted into my care to safely see you to your new home in Cannich. We are five days late... maybe more. Doubtless they fear the worst for us. Let's focus on the task at hand."

Katie raised an eyebrow and cocked her head at Theresa. "How far is this village?"

"I'm guessing about four or five miles as the crow flies."

"Fohget it." Katie dove back into her stew. "Too bloody far, an' how do you know there's a village nearby?"

Theresa cracked a small smile. "I went there after I... shot Tad. A woman took me in for a time. After that, they sent me to Saint Austin's."

"Why dint you stay in the village with the woman? Eh?"

"I was... a bit of trouble," Theresa replied. "I became cross with the woman's husband and... well, I took his rifle and shot their toilet— whilst he was still upon it." She shrugged. "I was an angry little girl."

Katie's eyes grew wide, and she smirked. "Remind me not to make you cross! You shoot people!"

Hilary broke her long silence. "What about Mina's dream? Isn't it dangerous for us to leave here? What about that man?"

"Mina said it was raining in her dream. We have half a foot of snow outside. I think we should be fine for a couple of days. But I also think it best to get as far away from here as possible and as soon as possible," Theresa said.

Theresa indulged herself in several pipefuls of stale tobacco and a mug of eighty-year-old wine after dinner. Mina had curled up into a ball on the floor, fast asleep. Hilary covered her with the wolfskins before turning to a game of *I spy with my little eye* with Katie.

Theresa continued to gaze at the wall, rocking back and forth in the old squeaky chair between puffs of tobacco. If she could only remember…

Mina's nightmare returned like a skip in a scratched record, playing the same lines over and over.

She again finds herself walking alone in an empty moorland, the cold rain soaking her to the bone, the rain stabbing her face with needles of ice. She walks aimlessly, her movements in slow motion.

She is dressed in Elvish clothing and a dark, hooded cloak. A small puddle of water sloshes around in her open hood as she walks. Her braided hair is matted to her head and face. Suddenly the man—his horrible bulging eyes and the stench of his breath are inches from her face.

He grasps her head with his hand, a hand now missing two fingers and wrapped in bloodied gauze. "Where is she?" he sneers.

Mina can feel her heart pounding in terror, pulsing through her body down to the ends of her fingertips as his words echo in her head.

She's now lying on her back in the mud, her eyes open, the rain pelting her face. She feels so cold as her lifeblood drains from her body. Her heartbeat is now so very faint that she can no longer feel it.

As darkness envelops her, a single word enters her ear in a whisper. She opens her eyes to the sound of a woman's voice calling her name. It's Theresa, kneeling above her; she's crying.

As Theresa gently cradles her head with her hand, Mina whispers in Theresa's ear, "I… would have liked… very much… to have been your daughter."

Darkness swallows her in silence, as the last breath leaves her body.

Chapter Two

Thomas

TOM WANDERED BAREFOOT and coatless in the storm after his failed attempt to rid himself of Theresa and her co-conspirators.

He sheltered in his broken-down motorcar during the worst of the storm, but being underdressed and without supplies, he eventually abandoned the car and followed the road back.

Blinded by the blizzard winds, Tom misjudged the road's shoulder where the drifting snow had created a false edge. He stepped off the edge and tumbled over twenty feet to the bottom of the ravine. Had the slope not been covered in so much snow, he would have been killed on the rocky surface beneath it.

Fortunately for Tom, only his nose was broken. But he was now trapped. Even in good weather, scaling the sheer wall would have been nearly impossible without proper climbing gear.

Only his anger and hatred gave him the will and strength to keep going. Frostbite had taken hold in his hands and feet. If he didn't find shelter soon, he would freeze to death here and likely never be found or, worse, find himself a meal for any wild beasts or birds living nearby. Tom pressed on through the night.

Just before dawn, his feet and hands nearly frozen, Tom stumbled into a small village. The stone buildings were covered in moss and vines and had thatched roofs of thick, dried peat dug and cut from the nearby bogs for insulation.

He staggered toward a building that looked much like a livestock stable. The door was unlocked, and he bulled his way in. In one of the empty stalls, he found several woollen horse blankets, though they smelled more like oxen, and promptly wrapped himself in them on the hay, desperate for warmth. He shivered violently as the blood began circulating in his body again. Soon he passed out from exhaustion.

Two children, Yavin and Moiré, quietly approached the stable, all bundled up in their coats, hats, scarves, and mittens.

Milking the goats was not their favourite task, but it was their turn. The goats were fussy and would nip at their ears and eat their hair, but in their village, everyone was expected to do their part.

Moiré stopped short as they reached the gate just outside the stable. It was open as was the stable door. Everyone knew it was their responsibility to keep the gate closed lest the animals escape or be attacked. The strange wolves had been coming down to this area more and more because of the long winter and scarcity of food. Losing even a few of their animals could devastate the little village.

The children carefully closed the gate behind them. Yavin looked at the ground below. Footprints led into the stable. As he started for the doorway, Moiré grasped his coat.

"Go tell your father that someone is in the stable," Moiré said. "I'll have a look-see."

"I'm the man here, and you're the girl! You should go!" he whispered in protest.

"I'm older than you, and he's *your* dad. I'm also quieter and less clumsy."

Yavin nodded reluctantly and set the wooden milk bucket down in the snow. "Be careful!" he whispered.

Moiré peered into the stable. An unpleasant smell like spoilt meat filled her nostrils. She crept in, looking into each stall for something out of place. The odour grew stronger the farther down the stable she moved. Moiré's eyes opened wide. A man was lying in the stall under the animal blankets. He looked fevered and grey. He was covered in perspiration and seemed to vibrate. Both his feet were sticking out of the blanket. His right foot and ankle were swollen and looked purple in colour. Several of his fingers looked blackened.

She realised the dreadful smell was coming from the man. Moiré's keen senses told her that something was very wrong, not just regarding the condition of the man, but something in the man himself. She sensed a darkness in him. She slowly backed away toward the door, feeling a bit sick inside.

Yavin, out of breath, met her at the door.

"They're on their way," he whispered.

"What did he say when you told him?" she whispered in return.

"Take a wild guess," he said with a smile.

She returned the smile to her blue-eyed friend. "Got bless it?"

Yavin nodded silently. "He also said for you to get the hell out of there."

They turned to see Yavin's father and several other men hurrying toward them, armed with rifles and clubs. Mitchell quietly shooed the children from the barn with a wave of his hand.

"Go!" he commanded in a whisper. Moiré hurried home, telling everyone along the way of the strange visitor in the stable.

Wick Mitchell was one of the leaders of the village and by far the most respected. His rugged appearance, whilst intimidating, was tempered with wisdom and levelheadedness. They often referred to him as the Sheriff.

The men entered the stable, holding their noses.

"He's got flesh rot, and it's spreading fast," one man said to Mitchell. "We'll have to act quickly!"

Mitchell looked at the man on the ground. "Poor sod. Wonder what happened to him."

The men wasted no time in bundling up the man and carrying him to the community gathering place.

Tom slipped in and out of consciousness from fever. With each awakening, he witnessed what seemed to be snippets from a book, as though he were flipping through a novel, reading an occasional sentence here and there, disjointed, yet still connected to the story as a whole. He could hear voices, but he couldn't understand the strange words, yet he was sure that the conversation must be about him.

Sometimes what he could see and hear would almost come into focus and sound close by. Other times the faces were blurred, and voices echoed in overlapping chaos, seeming to be very distant.

Tom came to realise that he was lying on his back, perhaps on a large table, with several people surrounding him, numerous candles lighting the room.

As he became more lucid, he began to look around the strange room. Turning his head to his left, he saw two small children peering through a doorway, watching him intently. Were they his enemies?

Suddenly Tom felt his right arm being pulled away from his side. He slowly turned his head to see why, blinking often to dispel the stinging sweat rolling into his eyes.

A man was placing someone's hand onto a wooden table much like the one Tom used in his butcher shop. Another man came into view, holding what looked like a small axe. They spoke to each other, but Tom couldn't understand their words.

What were they doing?

The man placed the axe just below the blackened portions of the fingers. He then smacked the back of it, severing the fingers from the hand. It reminded Tom of how he would cut off and discard sections of noticeably spoilt meat in the butcher shop in hopes that what remained could still be sold for profit.

Using a delicate knife, an old woman began scraping the remaining rotting tissue from the hand. Blood began flowing freely from the cleaned wounds.

Suddenly all Tom's senses returned in a flash as he was now completely conscious. Searing pain filled his hand and arm. It was *his* hand they were chopping!

Profanity spewed from Tom's mouth, and rage filled his heart as he struggled to free himself from these butchers. They were chopping him into pieces! They must be co-conspirators with Theresa, that old man and those horrible children! Tom grasped the old woman by the throat. Rage filled his eyes as he ripped the knife from her hand.

She yelled out words that sounded like gibberish to him.

The men struggled to restrain him as he slashed at them with the knife.

They bound him to the table with rope in seconds. It took two men to pry the knife from his bloodied hand. As he struggled, the old woman poured a bitter liquid down his throat. He coughed and choked but soon found himself very sleepy. The voices again echoed in his ears as Tom struggled to keep his eyes open.

He turned his head toward the two children cowering near the doorway in horror.

Moiré and Yavin felt an icy chill run up their spines as the man's hate-filled gaze bored into them. They quietly left, returning to their chores.

"Something not right about that one," Moiré said after a long silence.

Yavin nodded. "I don't understand why he seems so angry. He looked at us as though he wanted to hurt us. He has dreadful energy."

Moiré shivered at the thought of the man's face and red eyes. Just for a moment, the man reminded her of some paintings she had seen of a character called the devil from an old book she had read. Moiré shivered again.

Chapter Three

The Wall

THERESA STOOD BEFORE the rock wall, studying it for several minutes. Hilary quietly approached.

"Theresa," she said, "Mina is having another bad dream. Should I wake her?"

Theresa turned to see the small girl twitching and perspiring heavily on the floor. "No, Hils," she said. "Let her finish the dream. She woke before she finished it last time. It might be very important."

"Are we sleeping on this hard, cold floor tonight?" Hilary asked. "I'm so worried that Mina has taken ill."

Theresa smiled. "How would you like to sleep in a warm bed tonight, Hilary?"

Katie cut in, sounding left out and annoyed. "Oi! I heard that! Why does she geh to sleep in a warm bed? I want a warm bed too!"

"We will all sleep in warm beds tonight, Miss Katie!" Theresa said with a laugh.

With that, Theresa began feeling the left side of the wall, running her hand up and down the outer edge of the rock, fumbling for something unseen. After a moment, the girls heard a *click*, and the rock wall moved in slightly. Theresa pushed on the wall gently, and it opened, revealing a long, dark hallway. Above the round brick archway was a plaque written in Old Elvish.

"What does it say?" Hilary inquired.

"PORT OF TWO WORLDS," Theresa replied.

Retrieving an oil lamp from one of the nearby shelves, Theresa rolled the dried wick up and down into the lamp's reservoir to moisten it. After procuring several of the long matches, she then lit the lamp and held it up in the opening of the hidden hallway. It revealed a long tunnel cut deep into the hillside. The walls and ceilings were redbrick with rounded archways going down as far as the eye could see. Many rooms were on either side, trimmed in some exotic wood of a deep red colour. The round doors were reddish black and looked handcrafted. The floor was made of cobblestone, reminiscent of old London in the late eighteen hundreds.

Theresa smiled as she watched Hilary and Katie staring down the hallway, wide-eyed, in awe.

"Crikey… This isn't a cabin. It's an inn! No. A hotel!" Katie marvelled.

Behind them, Mina had awakened from her horrible dream and quietly crept up behind Theresa and the girls to see what had captured their attention.

Katie turned and looked closely at the girl. Mina's face was ashen and drenched in sweat. "You ole right?"

Mina shook her head and stared at the ground.

"Let's get you all to bed, especially Mina." Theresa put her arm around the shaking child.

"No. I don't want to sleep anymore… ever. I don't want to dream." Her voice trembled with fear.

Theresa led them down the corridor. "I wonder if these oil sconces still work." She struck a long match and held it to the centre of the torch on the wall. Nothing happened.

"Wait… now I remember." A small round toggle was inset just below the neck of each wall sconce. With her thumb, Theresa clicked it to the right, "One. Two. Three." She clicked it back to the left.

Holding the match above it again, it lit right up.

"Clever. Deposits just enough oil in the reservoir for the night, yeah?" Katie said with a raised eyebrow.

Theresa nodded. She lit several more sconces down the long brick corridor. The cold air was stale and musty. She opened the first two doors on the left and lit a lantern in each room.

Each bedroom had two beds with very ornate head and footboards. The headboards were sculpted to resemble some exotic animal from a type of metal that looked like iron painted black. Gold and copperleaf were somehow fused with the metal, creating incredibly fine details and making each animal look very realistic. The footboards were as beautifully crafted as the headboards, with intricately scrolled leaves and flowers embedded into the frame.

Beautiful tapestries hung on each wall, crafted from some strange glistening material, each depicting a forest or water scene. Numerous candles, a washbasin, wooden wardrobe, clothes dresser, and two chairs completed the room.

Theresa lifted the corners of the thick linen tarpaulins that covered the two beds, carefully gathering them by each corner, as they were filled with dust, revealing hand-quilted bedspreads beneath that were as beautiful as the tapestries.

"Right then," Theresa said cheerfully. "Katie, Hilary… this is your room tonight. Off to bed. It's very late."

"We'll freeze to death in here! I can see me breath," Katie protested. "There's only one blanket on this bed!"

Theresa seemed a bit annoyed. "No, you won't! Go on. Take to your bed. You'll see!"

Katie lifted the covers and peered within. "Are there bugs? I don't like bugs."

"Katie," Theresa said with impatience growing in her voice.

Katie raised her hand as though in school, wanting the teacher to call on her. She began tapping her foot impatiently as Theresa stared at her.

"Yes?" Theresa said in a slow monotone, folding her arms.

"Is there perchance a proper toilet I can use befoh I pop, or should I just squat an' pee roight here?"

"Down the hallway, second or third door on the right. Just don't fall in! It's a long way down to the bottom. You won't thank me if you do!"

After exchanging a look of fear with Hilary, Katie disappeared down the corridor.

Hilary and Mina looked longingly at Theresa, seeming to ask with their eyes if they could follow Katie.

"Off you pop," Theresa replied, rolling her eyes and shaking her head. Mina slowly staggered down the corridor behind them, swaying from side to side. Concern filled Theresa as she watched the frail child wobble toward the loo.

Katie and Hilary quietly crawled beneath the covers, though Katie could be heard mumbling under her breath, "I'll be found in the morning frozen solid with frost covering me cold dead body."

Theresa and Mina looked on as the two girls' eyes grew wide and smiles covered their faces.

"The bed's warm!" Hilary said excitedly.

"It's the elven material from which they're made. It will help you fall asleep quickly too!" Theresa said as she led Mina from the room.

Mina poked her head back around the doorway several seconds later. "G'night." But Katie and Hilary were already fast asleep.

After removing the tarpaulins from the two beds in the next room, Theresa bade Mina sit down.

"You had another bad dream?" she asked, already knowing the answer.

Mina nodded and hung her head. Theresa gently lifted Mina's chin so that the girl's eyes met hers. "Share it with me... all of it."

Mina shook her head and cried.

Theresa refused to take no for an answer. "Mina," she said sternly, "this is very important. Share your dream with me; I *must know* what you saw."

Mina frantically glanced around the room as though seeking a place to hide from the moment. After an awkward silence, she relented and nodded. She touched her two fingers to her forehead and, after a moment, placed them on Theresa's brow.

As she shared the vision, Mina's eyes filled with tears that rolled down her cheeks, staining them pink. The girl continued to sob as Theresa sat stunned and unable to look at the weeping child beside her.

Mina's final words in death, *I would have liked very much… to have been your daughter,* played in Theresa's mind over and over. She shook back the tears, unable to speak.

Not again. I can't…, Theresa thought, remembering Lucy, her lost daughter.

After a moment, she regained her composure. Theresa cradled Mina's face in her hands and looked deep into her eyes.

"Listen to me. We won't let that happen. Hear me? We *won't* let it happen!" A tear rolled down her own cheek as she spoke.

Theresa let Mina cry in her arms as she stroked her hair and held her close. After reassuring her several more times, she tucked her into bed and kissed her on the forehead, pulling the covers up close to her chin.

"Good night, Theresa," the little girl said, her eyes already getting heavy.

Theresa smiled. "Good night, Lucy."

She sat in the nearby chair, thinking, a blanket wrapped about her. She had much to consider and plan. Every detail must be worked out to perfection…

4 Chapter four

The Devil Inside

MINA AWOKE AFTER a dreamless night. As Theresa slept soundly in the bed next to hers, she rubbed her aching ear. The throbbing pain made her feel dizzy and a bit queasy. Unsure of the time, she quietly lifted her covers and crept out into the long corridor, tiptoeing on the cold cobblestone floor through the passageway into the cabin.

Light was streaming in around the damaged door and window frame. She carefully pulled the door open a few inches to see the morning light shining brightly. The snow was already melting, making the landscape soggy and wet.

Mina shivered as she closed the door. Her bed was quite warm, but the cabin was not. She could see her own breath as she hurried back to the bedroom, making a quick stop at the loo first. She crawled back under the covers to warm herself, letting out another shiver.

Theresa awoke, unsure of where she was for a moment.

"Everything okay, Mina?" she said sleepily.

Mina nodded and apologised for waking her.

"I wonder what time it is," Theresa said aloud but mostly to herself.

"It's morning. The sun is shining!" Mina said, trying to sound cheerful.

Theresa sat up, rubbed her stiff neck and aching shoulder, then let out a shiver of her own. "Right then. I'll make us a proper breakfast, and then we are off to town!" She tried to sound equally cheery.

Mina held Theresa's hand as they sauntered into the cabin. "I believe I saw a tin of dried oats in here. That should make a nice brekky for all of us. Shame we haven't milk or sugar though," Theresa said.

Mina wasn't looking at Theresa, so she didn't hear a word. Her focus was on the cold cast-iron stove that had kept them so warm the previous evening during the storm.

"Do you know how to turn this on, Theresa? I'm ever so cold."

Theresa set the cook pot and oats on the table. "Why don't you wake Hilary and Katie? Hils fired it up last night without a hitch. Have her do it, eh?"

Mina nodded and turned toward the door, then stopped. "Theresa?"

"Yes, love?" she said as she checked the container of oats for bugs.

"Why does that man want to kill me?" Mina's voice quivered with the question. "Is he a bounty hunter of the Tuatha or Firbolgs?"

Theresa looked into her eyes for a long moment. She bade Mina sit down at the table with her. After draping her coat on the little girl, she began.

"No, love, it's not about you. It's about me. Actually, it's about Thomas, my former husband. Even when Thomas was a young lad, his mum knew something wasn't right about him. He had a reputation in the fishing village where he grew up of strangling dogs and cats just so he could watch their faces as they died. He thought it funny. He was a cruel child. The fishermen and their families were afraid of him.

"When he was, oh, about eighteen, someone pinched his father's fishing boat, which is a major taboo in a fishing community where it's their livelihood. Thomas and his brother Jimmy were quite certain that it was the Dawsons and set out to get revenge. The Dawsons were a competing fishing family in the village. Thomas and Jimmy went over to Old Man Dawson's house and beat him with a club within an inch of his life. As a result, the old man had a stroke and never spoke or walked again. Old Man Dawson's three sons decided to return the favour and set out for the house of John Collins, Thomas's father. They planned to burn it to the ground. The news got back to Thomas and Jimmy, and they ambushed the three Dawson boys just outside their own property line… killed them all. A couple of weeks later, they realised the boat hadn't been pinched after all but that Jimmy had just forgotten to tie it off in the harbour. They found it adrift nearly a mile out to sea. They laughed and joked about it. No remorse whatsoever. Thomas was not only born without a soul but he was also born with something evil inside him, almost like a parasite, growing and wanting to get out. Jimmy is just as soulless, but in the end, he's just a coward who hides behind his big brother."

"Did you know all this when you married him?" Mina asked with wide eyes.

Theresa shook her head. "No. He could be quite the charmer. His mum came to me after she learned I was pregnant with our daughter. She urged me to get away from him, to get as far away as possible. His mother! I didn't listen. About seven or eight years later, Thomas killed my dog, Milton. He shot him in the head because he was a poor hunting dog, and he laughed about it. He also blamed me for the death of our daughter and gave me this." She pointed to the scar on her face.

"Your daughter is the blond girl," Mina said.

Theresa nodded. "Thomas is evil, Mina. So because you are with me, he wants to get rid of you too, same with Hilary and Katie. He sees all of us as the enemy. I am so sorry that I dragged all of you into this mess."

After an awkward moment of silence, Theresa stood and clapped her hands together, signalling it was time to change the subject.

"So, Mina! Wake Hilary and Katie, and we'll get breakfast on, yeah?"

Mina nodded and sauntered back to the girls' room to wake them, still wearing Theresa's huge coat draped over her shoulders, the ends of it dragging on the ground and leaving several lines in the dust behind her. Theresa stood watching as Mina disappeared into the long corridor. She smiled.

After a few moments, Theresa could hear the sound of hurried footsteps approaching from the corridor.

"They're gone!" Mina cried. "Hilary and Katie are gone!"

Theresa rushed to the missing girls' room with Mina close behind. She looked frantically about for any sign of Hilary and Katie. She felt the beds. They were cold. Theresa hurried over to the large wardrobe and opened the door to see if perchance the girls were hiding in it. She rustled through the old dusty clothes and cloaks hanging on hooks, but the girls were not inside.

Suddenly Theresa turned and hurried back up the brick corridor to the cabin door. Giving it a yank, she pulled it open and studied the snow on the ground before her. As the door faced north, the snow was unaffected by the warm sunshine and temperatures. There were no prints leading away; Hilary and Katie didn't leave through the front door.

Mina had finally caught up to Theresa, who stood deep in thought.

After a moment, Theresa looked at Mina with fear in her eyes. "Oh God. I know where they are!" They hurried down the brick corridor into the darkness.

Chapter Five

Katherine

KATHERINE OPENED HER eyes as she heard her mother mention her name. Her father and mother were having another heated conversation about her. She lifted her head from her pillow to peer out the car's windows. Katherine looked about her surroundings, recognising the landmarks; she could make out a small town in the distance, and beyond that lay the rolling hills that surrounded their family estate. They would be home soon. She lay back down, rubbing her face on the soft, plush pillow. She felt a little poke against her forehead and, using her freshly manicured fingernails, pulled a goose feather from the pillow. She studied it whilst her parents argued.

"This makes no sense, Charles, sending Katherine to boarding school just before the holidays. You know how she loves to decorate the Christmas trees and Christmas biscuits! All the other children will be home with their families except her. I find your decision ill-timed and insensitive. I demand you reconsider this!"

"We have servants to decorate the trees and handle the cooking chores. The decision has been made. This is the finest and most prestigious boarding school in England. The education Katherine will receive is second to none."

"She wants to focus on her music interests and science, not homemaking and societal etiquette!"

"Remember your place, Margaret! I will decide what her interests are. Not Katherine and certainly not you. I will tell her what to think. We will speak of this no further!"

"Pompous bastard," Margaret mumbled as she angrily slapped the side of the Rolls with one of her gloves. After a moment, she looked to the back seat where Katherine lay. Their eyes met.

She caressed her daughter's face with her hand, and Katherine smiled up at her.

"Would you please sit in your seat properly, Margaret?" Charles commanded. "We are nearly home. You look... undignified. What if someone should see you?"

Katherine's upper lip curled and an eye twitched at the sound of her father's voice.

Margaret froze in place as she read Katherine's reaction. Her eyes moved to her daughter's belly, which poked out from beneath the baggy dress she wore. It seemed bloated and twitched several times with strange ripples echoing outward like a stone tossed onto a still pond. Margaret placed her hand on it. She felt movement within.

She slowly turned her eyes to Charles, her face filling with fury. "That's why you didn't want her here. You couldn't hide what you've done. You were going to have them deal with your sin. You bastard. You bastard!" she screamed as she began striking him over and over.

Almost instantly, Charles lost control of the car. Missing a sharp right turn, it plummeted off the embankment, rolling several times.

Katherine opened her eyes in great discomfort as her mother pulled her from the wreckage. Suddenly the car burst into flames. Her father, trapped within, demanded Margaret help him instead of Katherine. Margaret collapsed onto the ground next to her daughter and wept.

"I'm so sorry, Katherine. Please forgive me, my love."

"It's not your fault, Mother," Katherine said in her very posh and refined accent as her father shrieked in agony as he was being consumed. "It was Father's. It was always Father's."

Margaret's eyes grew still.

"Mother? Mother? Mother!" Katherine cried out.

Suddenly a horrible pain crushed within her abdomen and then another and another. Katherine screamed as she felt something moving from within her, forcing its way out.

Blood began flowing, soaking her dress as the horrible, relentless contractions came faster and faster.

"Mother!" she cried out in desperation. "Help me! Mother!"

Katherine held her son in her arms. The tiny, blood-covered child lay motionless and was growing cold.

"A name... You need a proper name. Mother, what should I...?" Katherine looked again into her mother's lifeless eyes. "Daniel. I'll call you Daniel. I'm so sorry, Daniel."

The ground was far too hard to make a proper grave for her stillborn son and mother, so a pile of stones was the best she could do. Katherine sat in shock, too numb to cry. The sun journeyed from the east to the west but she remained motionless and unblinking, covered in her own blood, staring at the graves before her.

Katie stood. After warming her hands near the still smouldering motorcar, she turned and began walking toward the setting sun in a direction opposite of home.

Katie awoke, her heart racing and her breath coming in short gasps. "What an 'orrible dream!" she said in a quivering whisper, wiping away the tears.

Her bladder was gravely in need of being emptied. It was still quite dark as she hurried down the corridor toward the lavatory, the wall torches still blazing. She felt wide-awake and rested and surmised that dawn must be near.

After relieving herself, she crept back down the corridor but after a moment realised that she was going the wrong way as the torches farther down the long hallway weren't lit. Curiosity took hold of her, and she ventured into the darkness, feeling her way along the rough brick wall in the faint light.

Soon she came to a doorway at the far end of the corridor. This door differed from the rest, made of very old oak and cold to the touch.

She slowly opened it and poked her head inside. A putrid smell filled her nostrils as the damp air made her shiver.

"What 'ave we got here?" she mused aloud, staring into the darkness.

Katie hurried back up the brick corridor to her room.

"Oi, Hils! Wakey, wakey!" she said excitedly, shaking the sleeping Hilary.

"What's wrong?" Hilary popped up suddenly in her bed.

"Nuffin'!" Katie said with a big grin on her face. "I found sumpfin'!"

The girls quickly dressed. Hilary had just finished putting on her shoes when Katie grasped her by the hand and dragged her down the corridor toward the big oak door.

"You're going to get us in trouble again," Hils said as Katie lifted one of the torches from the wall.

"Nooo! Me? Never! Shut up!" Katie exclaimed as she turned the heavy handle on the door.

The torch lit the way as they descended the steep, narrow wooden stairs.

Hilary and Katie held their noses at the dreadful odour that surrounded them.

"Something quite foul down here," Hilary said as Katie lit the series of wall sconces every twenty steps or so. The walls were rock, and as each torch was lit, the cavern below revealed its vast size and secrets.

They reached a wood landing, which had a sharp, ninety-degree turn to it followed by many more stairs below, each one creaking as they stepped down upon them.

"Katie, we should go back. We shouldn't be down here. Theresa will be very cross," Hilary said with concern on her face.

"Oh, don't be such a chicken, Hils! What she—"

There was a loud *crack*, and Hilary let out a cry as a chunk of one of the old decaying steps snapped off, landing her on her bum with a thud. After a very long delay, they heard the bit of wood hit the ground below.

"You ole right?" Katie asked as Hilary righted herself and rubbed her sore bottom.

"These stairs are very narrow, and I nearly fell off the edge! We should go back! This place is decidedly unsafe!" Hilary said again, dusting herself off.

But Katie wasn't paying attention. Something had caught her eye.

"Look at that!" she said in awe.

The cavern was breathtaking. It was at least four stories tall and nearly as long and wide. Thousands of grey organic towers filled the perimeter of the cavern, with nearly an equal amount hanging down from the ceiling and forming the walls. The towers stood like soldiers with their arms raised, each one reaching into the ceiling and supporting its weight. They were each as big around as an oak tree and thrice as tall but were an octagon shape rather than rounded. A bluish hue emanated from the base of each tower, creating a dim light that filled the cavern.

The girls stood in stunned silence at the scene before them. At the bottom of the cavern, a large stretch of dark water was visible from their vantage point. They slowly made their way down the stairs to the wooden dock that hugged the edge of the still body of water.

Katie lit several more torches that were attached to wooden poles along the dock. Each lamp brought into focus what was before them.

"What is it?" Hilary asked with fear in her voice.

"Iz a boat… a *big* boat!" she exclaimed as she fearlessly approached the sea vessel. They looked in awe at where the mainmast had been broken off about ten feet from its base. Slivers of wood and torn sections of the awning and canvas remained on deck in a hopelessly jumbled pile.

"She's a bit… poorly," Hilary said in almost a whisper.

"Aye, she's been through a lot. I'd say her seafaring days are done. Hils, this is a tomb. The ship's tomb."

Hilary nodded.

After the last of the torches were lit, an even more surprising sight was before them; the vessel was lodged into the rock wall, nearly a fourth of it, almost as if it was part of the wall itself.

The boat rested in the water, appearing to have remained untouched for many years. Katie felt the edge of the boat where it had become lodged into the rock wall. The two had become one, blended together in some magical way.

"I'll wager this was the entrance to Mina's planeh," Katie said, her eyes still fixed on the blended rock and wooden boat.

"She's not from another *planet,* Katie! She's from another... um... world." Hilary's words revealed that neither of them truly understood what Mina's world was or where.

"What's the difference?" Katie said dismissively as she ascended the plank leading to the main deck. The plank between the ship and dock creaked ominously with each step as she crept up it. After a moment of hesitation, Hilary gingerly followed.

The ship differed greatly from anything they had seen either in person or in print. It had smooth, sleek lines with rounded, tapered edges that spoke of craftsmanship far beyond this world. Intricate wooden carvings and symbols, made from an almost white wood, were inlaid into the frame of the ship with seamless perfection. Even in the dim light, the sails were an iridescent white that seemed to sparkle.

Katie's eyes were drawn to a strange glow emanating from where the rock wall blended with the ship, near the end of the boat itself. It was an odd-looking line, arching downward on both ends. It seemed to be folded inward on itself and emitted a colour that didn't have a name. She couldn't even think of a colour to compare it to. "Looks like me old toothless Gran... frowning," Katie mumbled.

It seemed to be floating in the air, hovering about seven feet above her, and had a strange, wrinkled pooch at its centre.

Katie moved a wooden box beneath the pooch, climbed upon it, and gently touched the area, not knowing what to expect, but it felt like what she could only describe as pursed lips.

"'ave a look at this! I fink iz the entrance. Or the exit. Not shoh," Katie exclaimed.

Hilary hurried over to see her discovery, Katie giving her a hand up onto the box.

"This is... was... the opening that this ship came through," Hilary whispered.

"Shut up! That's what I just said!" Katie retorted, her arms flailing by her side.

"The sign said PORT OF TWO WORLDS," Hilary continued. "This used to open up into Mina's world! This isn't just a port! It's a portal! The ship isn't just stuck in the wall, it's stuck in *both* worlds. Part of it's still there. The rest is here. This… line is where the two worlds… are… sewn together. Right here." Hilary touched the rubbery centre.

"Sumpfin tells me this wasn't sewn up proper," Katie said. "People are going to notice a weird ship and a… frown. They'll figure it out. They'll figure out what it is. You'd fink they'd be more careful."

"You are so right. I think something went wrong. Maybe because the ship isn't in all the way, it couldn't close. The portal isn't completely sewn up. Mr Turly said that he and Theresa came here on this ship. Maybe Turly was supposed to send it back, but when Theresa shot him… he couldn't. Or… look at the condition of it. Something happened on the way here. Perhaps a battle? What happened to the crew? Maybe there was no one left to take it back."

"Boggles me brain, it does."

"You think it could be opened back up?"

"Maybe," Katie said with a nod.

Chapter Six

The Círtolthiel

T HE GIRLS BEGAN exploring every inch of the ship, eventually finding a hatchway to the captain's cabin below. After lighting a small oil lamp, which they had discovered in a cupboard, they looked about the plush cabin in awe; it seemed so much larger inside than it was on the outside.

The mildew and mould that covered the ship had not found its way inside the cabin; it was in perfect condition, and even the air smelled pure.

The walls seemed to be covered in a soft satin cloth, but when Hilary felt it with her hand, she realised it was actually part of the wall. It was an elegant wood, as hard as stone but as soft as a rose petal, and certainly not from this world.

The room was filled with strange objects, maps, and sculptures. Hilary's eyes fell upon a wooden box at the edge of the captain's bunk. It looked much like the steamer trunks she had seen in catalogues from a place called Sears and Roebuck. But this wood was unlike any she had ever seen. The grain was in strange swirls rather than a straight line like most woods. The colours were pale off-white, rust, and several others she didn't have a name for. She marvelled at how much depth there was in the wood. What must the tree have looked like? Hilary opened the lid carefully, the hinges squeaking in protest. Up went her left eyebrow.

"Katie," Hilary said in almost a whisper.

Both Katie's eyebrows went up at the sight before them; it was a weapons cache. It contained a leather shoulder satchel; several bows; two leather quivers filled with arrows; two swords and a dagger, each in a leather belt sheath; and numerous other items.

Each tool had been engraved with Elvish lettering and was a finely handcrafted work of art. Even the tips of the arrows were hand detailed with incredible craftsmanship.

There were also several wind instruments, one resembling a pan flute, another looking much like a seashell with odd notches and holes in it, which had been crafted into a wind instrument, perhaps for a child.

They found it curious that these beautiful musical instruments were in the same trunk as the weapons.

Hilary smirked as Katie fondled the strange shell with wild eyes, turning it round and round, peering into all the holes, not sure of which end to blow into or even what it was, before turning her attention and smile toward the weapons.

A nearby wardrobe was filled with peculiar clothing that reminded Katie of what she had read about pirate ships and the odd threads they wore.

Katie quickly donned the oversized apparel as Hilary kept her hand over her mouth in a failed attempt not to laugh.

Soon Hilary was also dressed in the strange stitches, and the two girls found themselves on deck, playing Mutiny on the Bounty.

Katie took the role of the first mate who had mutinied against Captain Hilary. Even her pirate's accent was top-notch, flavoured with numerous *arrgs!*, *ois!*, and *mateys!* Her short stature, oversized clothes, and sword dragging on the ground behind her undermined the role she was playing so well. The hat she wore was three sizes too large and kept falling over and covering her entire head as she barked out orders to an imaginary crew who trembled at her authority.

Neither girl could remember having so much fun and quickly lost track of time.

"Oi! Cap'n 'ilary! We, the crew of this fine ship 'ave decided a change is due… Arrg! So iz time fer ye to walk the plank!"

Katie pulled her sword from its sheath with great difficulty, nearly losing her balance and toppling overboard. The razor-sharp metal glinted as she held it over her head.

"Argh!" she cried out again as Hilary giggled, pretending to have her hands tied behind her back. Hilary, in her best dramatic fashion, tried to look sombre as she headed toward the plank, which was nothing more than the walkway onto the wooden dock. "Walk the plank, ye scurvy!" Katie cried.

Suddenly the girls heard echoing footfalls coming down the stairway. It was Theresa with Mina not far behind. They could see the anger on Theresa's face.

"Off the boat!" Theresa commanded. "Off the boat now!" Her words echoed throughout the cavern and repeated over and over for what seemed like a full minute. Her voice was angry, and yet there was something beneath it. She sounded terrified. Theresa was nearly halfway down the stairway, and there was no way out for Katie and Hilary as she would be on them in less than two minutes. Mina followed behind as fast as her legs would carry her.

Katie sighed with a look of disgust, tossing her hat onto the deck. "Brilliant. It's the potty poopah," she mumbled aloud.

Hilary, on the other hand, looked mortified.

The girls slowly moved toward the wooden dock. As Hilary walked down the plank, she heard a *creak* below her feet between the ship and the wooden dock.

Katie followed behind, almost in her steps, the end of her sword dragging behind her in its sheath, carving a deep line into the wooden deck as she shuffled toward the dock.

As Katie stepped onto the plank, a loud *crack* sounded beneath her. Suddenly it gave way, splitting apart. Katie let out a scream as she plunged into the dead, black water.

"Katie!" Hilary cried out. "Katie!"

Katie was gone.

7 Chapter Seven

The Dead Water

MORE THAN A minute had passed since Katie's disappearance. It seemed like hours to Hilary as she stood by helplessly, fear for her friend's life growing with every passing second.

Theresa reached the cavern's floor and rushed to the water's edge. A few slimy bubbles made their way to the surface, popping slowly between the dock and the *Círtolthiel*, indicating where Katie had fallen in.

"Why isn't she coming up?" Hilary gasped. "Katie's a splendid swimmer! Why isn't she coming up? Oh my God! Oh my God!"

Theresa kicked off her shoes and pulled off her socks as she prepared to follow Katie in.

Suddenly Mina charged past them, diving straight into the still pool.

"Mina! No!" Theresa screamed, but it was too late. Within moments, the water stilled and became like glass, leaving no trace of either girl except for a single bubble.

Mina struggled to draw air into her lungs as there was almost none in the black water. Her webbed toes helped her to move quickly, but to where? Her ears were as useless beneath the water as they were above.

She continued swimming downward from the last position she had seen Katie, hoping the weight of the sword, the heavy clothes, and the thick leather belt were taking her down in a straight line.

Mina froze in place for a moment, trying to sense any movement near her in the blackness. A slight current of movement touched her hair.

She followed the motion, diving downward as several bubbles brushed against her face.

After a moment, Mina grasped Katie's motionless foot in the darkness, then felt her way up to Katie's head and face.

Katie was still and seemed to be stuck on something. Mina, with all her might, drew in air from the rancid water, then breathed it into Katie's mouth, drawing away the water that had filled Katie's lungs.

Nothing happened; Katie remained motionless. Mina, again with great effort, drew oxygen into her lungs and breathed it into Katie's mouth.

Katie began lurching frantically. Mina placed two fingers on Katie's forehead, sharing a single thought with her: *Mina.* Katie stopped thrashing.

Mina shared one more breath with Katie at her own expense. She now felt very queasy from breathing in the rancid water. Her heart pounded angrily in her chest, worse than ever before.

Mina worked her way down to find what was holding Katie in place. The weight of the sword had pulled Katie nearly fifteen feet below the surface of the water before becoming wedged between two columns that rose up from below.

Mina set to work loosening the belt from Katie's waist. The slimy water had made the leather stiff and slippery, and Mina's small hands struggled to free the belt post from its hole. After several attempts, it finally came free.

Katie wriggled out of the clothes, and the two girls ascended toward the dim light above. When Mina slowed and eventually stopped swimming, unable to go any farther, Katie grasped her by the collar and dragged her upward to the surface.

Theresa and Hilary quickly pulled the girls from the water. Katie coughed up vile liquid for several minutes before finally sitting up.

Mina, however, looked ghostly pale and weak. Every breath seemed to be a struggle for her. A sick feeling filled the pit of Theresa's stomach as she tried to comfort her. She checked Mina's pulse. Her heart was racing so fast there was scarcely a pause between the beats, and Melody's words about Mina's heart condition replayed in Theresa's mind.

"Come on, Mina. Let's get you upstairs," Theresa said softly, trying to disguise her concern.

Mina struggled to her feet, clearly disoriented, and turned toward the stairs with Theresa's arms around her for support.

One step, two steps, three... Suddenly the child crumpled to the ground, face-first.

"Mina!" Theresa rolled the girl onto her back. Mina's face was grey, her skin cold and clammy. Pulsating purple and blue veins branched across her face and neck like lightning in the sky, and her eyes appeared to be sunken into her skull.

Theresa checked her pulse again; the pounding rhythm was now very erratic.

Hilary and Katie held their breath in silence, their faces revealing the terror they felt within.

Theresa gathered the little girl in her arms and hurried toward the stairway with Hilary and Katie following behind.

Theresa led them into the loo and bade Hilary run a warm bath in the cast-iron tub. A hot spring ran beneath the ground, and the builder of the dwelling had tapped into it.

The water ran red from rust for a moment but soon cleared and became quite warm. Hilary placed the rubber stopper into the drain, and the tub began filling.

In the corner, Katie sat with her head on her knees, sobbing uncontrollably. "Oh my God, I've killed Mina! Iz ole me fault... I've killed Mina!"

Theresa placed her ear to Mina's lips to check her breathing; she wasn't.

Theresa lifted her up, the child's legs dragging limply on the stone floor, and wrapped her arms around Mina's stomach. She squeezed hard.

Mina vomited more than a litre of the black water onto the floor; the smell was absolutely revolting, but she opened her eyes. Theresa held her close as the girl began shaking violently.

With the tub filled, Theresa stripped the slimy clothing from Mina and slid her into the warm bath. She continued to shiver, but the warm water soon calmed her.

Theresa, Katie, and Hilary became fixated on Mina's legs, now enveloped with flesh-coloured fish scales.

"Hilary," Theresa said, "run into the cabin and fetch the jar of sea salt."

She nodded and scurried off, soon returning with the container, a look of puzzlement on her face.

Theresa smiled and handed the jar to Mina, who seemed quite eager to take it. She dumped most of it in her bathwater and dissolved it with her hands by swishing it around against the edge of the tub. Soon she submerged her head in the water and closed her eyes.

"Tha's. Not. No'mal," Katie remarked with a sob, still trying to regain her composure.

Theresa sat back against the wall and closed her eyes. "That was close," she said to herself.

Soon colour returned to Mina's face and body. She opened her eyes for a moment and smiled up at Katie, who began crying again.

Theresa sat with her head resting on her knees for nearly twenty minutes. Hilary and Katie sat quietly as well, lost in their own thoughts about what had just happened.

Katie's slimy clothes had nearly dried and were now firmly stuck to her skin. Her hair was greasy and matted to her head. She wanted to say something about how cold and grimy she felt but held her tongue, fearing she might awaken Theresa's anger prematurely, an anger that was sure to come.

Finally Theresa opened her eyes and spoke. She had been deep in thought.

"Hilary, would you mind going to the wardrobe in your room and seeing if there are enough clothes for the three of you?"

Hilary nodded and stood up.

Theresa then added, "Afterwards, please light up the stove so I can make us some breakfast." Hilary nodded again and dashed out of the room.

Theresa's eyes moved to Katie. "Do you understand what almost happened, Katie?"

The girl nodded slowly.

"Do you realise she drew all the toxins in that water from you into herself? She poisoned herself to save you."

Katie's eyes flooded with tears again as she began sobbing silently.

Theresa let out a long sigh as if releasing something unpleasant from within. She looked at her hands and clothes, covered in slimy residue. After filling a porcelain basin with water from the hand pump, she washed her hands and face, then cleaned the vomit-covered floor and laid a fresh towel down so it wouldn't be slippery. Theresa then moved toward the tub. Reaching into the now-cool water, she gently shook Mina's shoulder.

Mina opened her eyes and slowly sat up. She still looked ill but in much better spirits.

Theresa first checked the girl's pulse, then gathered a fresh flannel from the cupboard and helped her clean the sticky black goo off her body and face. She washed and rinsed Mina's hair, finishing off the old dried and cracked bar of soap that had sat undisturbed on the soap dish for over thirty years.

Theresa realised that she, in fact, had been the last one to use this tub when she was just a child herself. The last time she used that particular bar of soap, she was younger than Mina.

Hilary returned with three sets of clothes that were old and a bit musty-smelling but in excellent condition.

Theresa retrieved a soft towel and bade Mina leave the tub, drying her off as the girl leaned against Theresa's hip for support. Magically, the fish scales on Mina's legs and webbing between her toes receded when the towel removed the water.

Theresa helped Mina dress in the odd outfit, the girl still shivering a bit. She rolled the long trousers and sleeves up to the proper length as Mina giggled at her appearance in the nearby mirror.

"Trousers!" Mina announced in a weak but cheery tone. Theresa smiled.

"Your turn, Katie!" Theresa tried to sound more cheerful. "Into the bath with you, and don't forget to wash your hair!"

Katie complied silently, first rinsing the scum from the tub. It was sticky and difficult to remove. Normally, she would have made some sarcastic remark to lighten the awkward moment, but today she remained silent.

As Theresa handed her a fresh bar of soap from the cupboard, Katie tried to smile but failed as she realised Theresa was still cross with her. "You're not going to shoot me, are you?" Katie joked.

Theresa ignored her.

As the tub filled with warm water, Theresa rummaged through a drawer below the cupboard and found a hairbrush and wide-tooth comb. She closed the wooden toilet seat, quietly gathered Mina onto her lap, and began combing out the tangled mess of hair with the comb. Mina fumbled with the brush, expressing an occasional "Ow!" from the tangles as she rubbed its soft bristles against the back of her hands.

"You were very brave," Theresa said. "You saved Katie's life."

"I know," Mina said matter-of-factly. "She's my friend; she would have done the same for— Owww!" Mina winced again as the comb found another snag in her hair.

Katie's face contorted at Mina's words.

"Sorry," Theresa said quietly. "Your hair is a rat's nest!"

"Rats?" Katie said with a big grin. "Mina has rats living in her hair!"

Theresa paused for a moment and gave her the eye, at which Katie slowly and comically slunk down into the water, disappearing from view. *Blub, blub, blub.* Theresa rolled her eyes and shook her head, smiling slightly at Katie's attempt to lighten the mood.

After several moments, Theresa lifted her eyes back to Katie, who was now sitting in the tub, slathering herself with soap.

"Katie, do you have anything to say to Mina?" Theresa said, her eyes burrowing deep into Katie's soul. She tapped Mina's arm to get her attention and then pointed to Katie.

Katie squirmed in the tub at the obvious question. "Aye," she said. There was a long pause as she seemed to ponder the perfect response. "I can't believe you kissed me in the wotah. On the lips!"

Anger flashed in Theresa's eyes at Katie's words, but Mina screwed her face up into weird contortions and tossed the hairbrush at Katie's head.

"I wasn't kissing you!" Mina retorted as both girls began laughing.

Theresa's anger was replaced with a smile. Even now the children could laugh.

The girls giggled and joked back and forth for several minutes.

"Okay, enough, you two," Theresa said with a smile as she tossed Katie a towel.

Katie stood and began drying herself off. Suddenly something caught Theresa's eye, and the smile vanished from her face. Katie's abdomen was covered in stretch marks. Katie hurriedly wrapped the towel about her when she realised what Theresa was staring at.

"Katie?"

"Theresa, do you smell smoke?"

Theresa realised that smoke was indeed wafting down the corridor from the cabin. She plopped Mina onto her feet and rushed to the doorway.

Theresa could hear Hilary coughing and gasping for breath in the cabin. She closed the bathroom door behind her and disappeared into the black smoke, holding the collar of her flannel shirt over her mouth and nose as she felt her way along the brick wall.

Chapter Eight

Shipwreck of Memories

T HERESA FOLLOWED THE sound of coughing through the smoke and found Hilary, who had just managed to open the front door. Light streamed into the smoke-filled room.

"So sorry!" Hilary exclaimed out of breath from coughing. "I forgot I had opened the flue on the stove last night, so I accidentally closed it. It's open now. I'm sorry!"

Theresa plopped down in the rocking chair, relieved, as the smoke escaped through the front door. "I need a holiday," she muttered.

She loaded her pipe, filled a mug with stout, and quietly calmed herself by rocking in the old chair for several minutes, breathing deeply.

Soon the stove was hot, and the cabin warmed nicely. Before mixing the oatmeal with water, Theresa gave Hilary a hug and thanked her for her effort.

Katie and Mina soon crept in, still unsure if it was safe to enter.

"It's okay, girls. Come on in!" Theresa said, having forgotten that she had left them in the lavatory. She did her best to sound cheerful, though inside she felt totally knackered.

She turned to Hilary as Mina and Katie quietly seated themselves at the old wooden table. "Hils, you have enough time to take a quick bath if you like whilst I prepare this, so why don't you have a wash?"

Hilary was eager to comply as she was covered in soot and smelled of coal smoke.

The breakfast was filling and tasty, as Katie had found a container of hard brown sugar they could chip off and dissolve into their hot oatmeal. Katie also found a container of something resembling coffee and prepared it using a flannel to filter it through into her usual tar-like consistency. Theresa smiled, thinking back to when Katie stood before her, vibrating with a big grin on her face from having drunk nearly the entire pot of the thick brew in Tad's home.

Her thoughts moved to Tad and the sacrifice he had made for them. She missed his enormous nose and wild hair, but mostly his kindness. She had only known her uncle for a short time, but her memories would be with her for the rest of her life.

After they cleaned up the breakfast dishes and tidied up, Theresa informed the others that they would spend one more night at the cabin so Mina could recover from the morning's disaster. After putting Mina to bed, Theresa rummaged through her wardrobe and found a clean set of clothes for herself as well as a surprise—her old outfit from over thirty years ago, the very clothes she wore as she journeyed to this world on the *Cirtolthiel,* the ship that nearly cost her the lives of Katie and Mina. She smelled the fabric and held them close.

They were just the right size for Mina. After quietly laying them on the end of the sleeping girl's bed, Theresa indulged herself in a hot bath, filled with bubbles from the bar of soap she held under the stream of water as it ran, and several candles to lend a glow to the room. It felt so good to relax, even for a few brief moments.

After a dinner of vegetable soup and barley, the girls brushed their teeth from the large supply of toothbrushes and tooth powder that Katie had discovered in a cupboard, and then Theresa tucked them into their beds.

Once she was certain they were sound asleep, she descended the long staircase alone. The torches along the wall flickered in an eerie fashion as she approached her destination. She paused to study the *Cirtolthiel,* the ship that had brought her to this world against her will.

A cold shiver enveloped her as the ship before her began to move violently. It was tossed about like a rag doll in a dog's mouth by the angry ocean waves and massive walls of water rising up the port side and stern. Ear-splitting thunder and blinding lightning made her ears ring and the hairs on her neck and arms stand on end. The salty ocean spray stung her eyes and chilled her to the bone. A swell of water lifted the bow of the Círtolthiel *high into the air, then dropped it suddenly, before another wave caught it from below and began to roll it wildly from side to side. Theresa held her breath as cascading water engulfed the hull of the ship. An immense pressure bore down on them from beneath, threatening to tear them apart. In the flashing darkness, she could see Tad desperately tying her younger self to the base of the mainmast as the ship's captain and two remaining deckhands were washed into the sea. The ship rocked viciously, nearly tossing Tad overboard. Treena cursed and spit at her uncle, screaming nonstop for her father. Tad's long brown hair and black beard whipped about his face, stabbing him in the eyes relentlessly.*

Tad, looking deathly ill, vomited multiple times over the railing onto the deck below, much of it blowing back into his face and beard. He lifted his head. Theresa felt his eyes lock onto hers as she stood on the wooden dock. Theresa? *he mouthed. He then shouted something, and she strained to hear over the roar of the ocean and wind. "Theresa! Tell! Colin! I love him! Theresa! Tell Colin, I love him!" Theresa shivered, a chill dancing up her spine. Could Tad actually see her?*

He tied a rope around his ankle and to the railing, then looked back to see a massive wall of water bearing down upon himself and Treena, snapping the mainmast in two. The mast crashed onto the deck and railing, splintering and exploding as though a cannonball had struck it, nearly taking Treena's head with it.

Through the stinging ocean spray, Treena watched as her uncle, wrapped in the tangled rigging, was wrenched overboard by the furious wave.

She was now alone, tied to a broken wooden pole on a broken wooden ship.

After what seemed like hours, the ocean settled, and Treena set her eyes upon the setting moon. Silence filled her ears. She began humming the Old Song, her eyes still fixed on the moon. In the waning moonlight, as the grey ocean mist began veiling everything about her, she saw something moving. Something... was climbing over the edge of the ship and inching its way toward her... ever so slowly. Was it a probing tentacle of the Kraken come to take her to a watery grave? Treena held her breath, her heart pounding like a drum. As it rose up through the mist before her, Treena shrieked in terror.

With trembling hands, Tad released Treena from her bonds before collapsing onto the deck.

Theresa boarded the *Cirtolthiel*. With emotions and memories still flooding her mind, she toured it in silence, running her hands and fingertips along the edges of the ship, the railings, the wheel, the remnants of the mainmast, and the rope at its base. After a time, she made her way into the captain's quarters, closing the door behind her.

Chapter Nine

Elven Clothing

THE MORNING BROUGHT sunshine and warm temperatures as the three girls and Theresa prepared to leave their refuge for a town that Theresa scarcely remembered.

Katie browbeat Theresa for nearly an hour in protest of having to walk to town, claiming she needed rest.

After Theresa's stern lecture and reminder of the previous day, Katie eventually quieted herself and offered a meek, "Yes, Miss."

The four were dressed in earth-toned clothing from another world—light tan trousers, medium-brown or cream-coloured shirts—except for Mina, whose blouse was a deep green colour with brown stitching that had been crafted many years ago by Theresa's mother, Miramanee.

Theresa, Hilary, and Katie each donned a dark brown hooded cloak. The outer garments would have been only knee-long to an elf but nearly reached the ground on the girls, looking more like robes. The sleeves and trouser legs were rolled several times on Katie and Hilary to allow them access to their hands and feet.

As Mina donned Theresa's old cloak, she stared down at it for a prolonged moment, remembering the horrible dream from several nights before. Theresa gently lifted Mina's chin, and their eyes met.

"What is it, Mina?" Theresa said. "Don't you like it? My mum made that cloak for me when I was a little girl. In fact, she made the entire outfit you're wearing. It fits you perfectly!"

Mina's heart sank, as this was the very clothing she was wearing when she died. She also realised that she had not dreamt since that night. Was that to have been her last dream? Was she no longer dreaming because her life was to end soon?

"I think they're beautiful, Theresa. I just don't feel terribly well." She smiled politely, choosing not to say anything more about it.

"Mina," Theresa said as she knelt and fastened the button on Mina's cloak, "did Mr Turly ever mention someone named Colin?"

"Um... yes. He had a son. I think his name was Colin. Why?"

"No reason, love. I've just been thinking about him. Wondered if he had a family he left behind." Theresa kept her bizarre vision close to her heart.

"I think Colin died. Didn't say how, just that he died," Mina replied sadly. "Mr Turly would have been a wonderful father... don't you know."

"He would have been brilliant!" Theresa said with a smile, squeezing Mina's shoulders.

"You'd be a wonderful mother," Mina said with pleading eyes.

Theresa lowered her gaze and turned away.

As they ventured from the cabin toward the village some distance away, Mina noticed something had changed. Theresa was shouldering a leather satchel; she hadn't seen that in her dream. Did it mean something, or was it just a detail that she had overlooked?

The snow had nearly melted away, leaving behind a sticky squidge they would have to trudge through until reaching the rolling hills and forest beyond that. It was nearly midday when they ascended the last hill before the descent into the village below. A thick, dark forested area was to the east, the trees massive and dense. Hilary shuddered as she looked at them.

The troop of four stood at the top of the hill, looking at the valley below.

"The village is down there," Theresa said. "I think."

"All I see is dead grass, rocks, and bogs," Katie commented.

"It's there," Theresa reiterated. "It's just kinda… hidden."

"'ow do you hide an entire village?" Katie asked sarcastically.

"Very… carefully?" Theresa replied with raised eyebrows and a lopsided grin. "We have to stay centre of these large rocks on either side. Somehow they are the footpath to the village. If we stray from the path, we'll miss the village entirely. That's how they keep this place hidden."

"This lot sounds paranoid, if you ask me," Katie replied.

The sunny skies were giving way to grey and ominous clouds to the north. Arctic winds gave warning of an approaching storm. The girls were complaining of thirst and hunger when the pale and fevered Mina stopped in her tracks and warned them to go no farther.

Before them, in the path leading to the village below, the ground was covered in orchids… black orchids… harbingers.

Suddenly Mina collapsed to the ground, unconscious.

Chapter Ten

The Bridge Between Worlds

M OIRÉ PEERED OUT the window and scanned the area for any sign of the man. He had become quite unpopular in the week or so that he had spent amongst them. The darkness and cruelty emanating from within him seemed to grow each day. He would threaten and steal the villagers' food and spent most of his time in the stable, drinking sour mead nicked from the community supply house.

Rumours were sprouting up about the black flowers surrounding the village. Many said they were an omen about the man and that he should be banished immediately.

A closed town meeting was to be held that evening to discuss what to do with the stranger. His injuries were healing unnaturally fast, and many felt it was time for him to leave.

Moiré was relieved that there was no sign of him stumbling about the streets in a drunken stupor today. She wanted to spend some time with Yavin. They had seen little of each other over the past week as the adults had taken over stable chores for fear of the man. As she was about to venture out, she noticed something coming down the hill… people, an adult woman carrying a child and two older children alongside her. They were walking through the black flowers toward the village.

"Mum!" Moiré cried out. "Mum, you need to see this!"

An elderly woman who seemed much too old to be Moiré's mother hurried into the room. "What is it, love?"

The old woman's face grew fearful and grim as she peered out the small window. "Elves," she mumbled as she hurried out the door toward the strangers.

Moiré followed behind her. Elves had not visited the village for almost forty years now.

The old woman approached the strangers, stopping short of the line of black flowers, which she dared not cross.

"Elves *bhfuil tú?*" the woman demanded.

Theresa froze in place; she had not heard this language in many years. She searched her mind for the right words, and as the old woman studied them, her eyes grew wide at the sight of Mina's pointed ears.

"Um… *le do thoil… Ní mór dúinn do chabhair. An mbeidh tú cabhrú linn… le do thoil?*" Theresa said, pleading with the woman.

Nodding, the woman motioned them to follow.

As they entered the village, their eyes grew wide at the sights before them. Odd oxen-like animals with long woolly coats and horns made unusual humming and honking sounds as if to greet the strangers. A marketplace in the town square displayed curious styles of clothing reminiscent of what peasants would have worn during the Middle Ages and offered up strange, dried vegetables, meats, and fruits.

In the distance, they saw many villagers tilling and turning the ground for spring planting and ploughs being pulled by the strange beasts. Several small birds, chicken-like, with small, serrated teeth embedded into their beaks, clucked, clicked and scurried out of the way as they approached the home of the old woman and child.

"I fink we jus' made a left turn into the twelfth century," Katie whispered to Hilary, who nodded.

The house they entered was made of stone and covered with thick moss. These camouflaged dwellings would be easily overlooked by anyone casually walking by as the entire village seemed to blend in with its surroundings. The moss-covered door was low and even Katie and Hilary had to stoop to enter the house. The old woman pointed to a wooden hall tree. The visitors removed their cloaks and shoes, hanging them on hooks on the tree.

All around them, the walls were alive with greenery, the odd-looking plants reaching toward them with a strange curiosity. The air was thick, and damp. The smell of earth filled the room. As their eyes adjusted to the dim light, they noticed that the furniture in the house was spartan, but well-crafted. Their footsteps were muffled by the thick green moss that covered the floor.

They followed the woman down an arched hallway into a bedroom.

Moiré cleared off her bed, and Theresa set the sweat-drenched Mina upon it.

"Are they elves Mum? Moiré asked.

"Cén fáth a bhfuil tú anseo? Níor thug elves cuairt orainn le blianta fada," the woman demanded of the strangers.

Theresa's mind scrambled to understand the woman's words.

"Tá Mina *tinn go leor. Táimid tar éis siúl go leor... lá... go leor..."* Theresa searched her mind, but she could go no further. She simply couldn't remember the language. "Do you speak any English?" she finally asked in desperation.

The woman stared at her for a long moment. "I speak... Have we met before?" she said with great suspicion, her eyes squinting tight at the woman before her.

"Please... we need your help. Mina is very ill."

The old woman studied the four strangers before her, then pointed at Mina. "She is elf-kind. The rest of you are not," she stated firmly. "Yet you dress as elf-kind. What is this poor deception?"

Theresa took a deep breath, fearing that if she used the wrong words, the woman would turn them away. Pointing at each girl, she spoke slowly. "This is Hilary, Katie, and Mina. I'm Theresa."

The old woman studied Theresa with suspicion still in her eyes. "That doorway was closed long ago. She cannot be here. You speak as a Londoner, but I know you."

Theresa bit her lip at the woman's words. She remembered the old woman from many years ago, though she couldn't believe she could still be alive after all these years, virtually unchanged. The woman's name was Chloe, and she was the one who had taken her in after she ran away from Tad. She was known for taking in strays, and Theresa suspected that the young girl, who was calling her Mum, was perhaps another orphan the woman had adopted as her own. Chloe was a stern woman but had a kind heart, especially for children.

Their relationship had ended badly as it was Chloe's husband Theresa tried to shoot whilst he occupied the toilet. She hoped the woman wouldn't remember her.

She stared at Theresa for a long moment, the wrinkles around her leathered eyes creasing deeply.

"What's wrong with the elf?" the woman demanded in a fast, flat tone.

Katie spoke up. "Actually, she's only paht—"

"It's her ear actually, both of them," Theresa replied, quite relieved that the topic of conversation had turned back to Mina. "She was in London during a German air raid. The bombing silenced her left ear. Recently we were stranded by the snowstorm, and she lost the hearing in her right ear as well. I fear infection. She has a growing fever from a fall into some... foul water."

"An elf in London?" the woman mumbled to herself, shaking her head in disbelief.

"Actually, she's only paht—" Katie tried to interject again.

Theresa gave her a glare that could melt paint off an old barn. She returned Theresa's look with one of puzzlement.

The woman looked over the three children for a long moment before turning her attention to Mina.

"Moiré, *beir an lampa ola ón gcistin*," she said as she peered intently into Mina's seeping ear.

Moiré nodded and disappeared into the back room. Chloe felt Mina's forehead and neck, her face showing obvious concern at the heat radiating from the girl. She used a hollow metal tube flared at both ends to listen to the rhythm of Mina's heart, then let out a deep sigh, shaking her head.

Moiré returned with the small lamp already lit. After instructing Moiré to hold the lamp near Mina's ear for illumination, the woman lifted a small, round piece of glass from a string around her neck through which she peered deeply into the unconscious child's ears.

She sat in thought for a long moment and then left the room without a word, soon returning with a wooden box of various dried herbs and a container of thick, clear liquid in a glass vial.

After carefully measuring out several pinches of differing herbs, including a snipping of a pale green plant from one of the living walls, she instructed Moiré to grind them into thick paste using a porcelain mortar and pestle. The woman mixed four drops of the thick liquid into the mix and drew it into a glass dropper.

Mina awoke momentarily to the stinging liquid being dripped into her ear and tried to pull away. Theresa gently grasped her shoulders and reassured her it was all right, calming her fear. The delirious child again slipped into unconsciousness.

After applying three drops to each of Mina's ears, the woman packed them tightly with wads of cotton.

"That is all I can do for now," the old woman said.

"*Tá sí an-te mháthair*," Moiré said.

Chloe nodded. After giving Moiré instructions, the girl left the room to gather a bowl of cool water and a clean flannel to calm Mina's fever.

"We'll let her rest a bit," the woman said. "I'll put on the kettle, and we'll have a cup of tea and a bite to eat. I'm sure you're all hungry and thirsty after your journey here, and I have questions. First off, where did you walk here from, and what on God's green earth were you thinking crossing the black harbingers? That was very foolish!"

Theresa hadn't anticipated that question. The port of two worlds was never to be spoken of to anyone from this world, but this woman obviously knew of it.

"It's a very long story, Chloe, but the past few days we have been staying at a cabin a few hours' walk from here. But thank you so much for your kindness. We truly are grateful."

The woman stared into Theresa's eyes, the look of suspicion returning. "You were at the *Wait*? I was the caretaker there for many years. And how do you know my name? I haven't told you yet!"

Silence filled the room. Theresa suddenly felt very flushed and hot.

"Oh shit, she's on to you, T'reeza," Katie mumbled, followed by a quick elbow in the ribs from Hilary.

"Theresa…," Chloe muttered. "That's what threw me off. That's not your name, is it? And your accent?" Her eyes squinted tight again.

Theresa stood silent.

"Theresa… Theresa… Treena! That's your name, isn't it?" the old woman demanded with a wagging index finger. "I remember you now. You shot my husband!"

"Shot at," Theresa confessed. "I didn't actually shoot him!"

The old woman stared at Theresa for a long moment, then suddenly the deep creases around her eyes faded, and a big smile spread across her face. "You owe me a toilet!"

Relief filled Theresa's heart as she let out a deep breath. She hadn't realised that she had been holding it for nearly a minute.

"It's a shame you didn't finish off that bastard!" the old woman said, joking.

A smile crept across Theresa's face. "You're… not angry?"

"Heavens no. That old whore was bedding half the women in the village! It was the best day of my life when you ran that tosser off." She laughed, returning Theresa's smile.

As the kettle heated, Theresa enjoyed her pipe at the kitchen table. Chloe refused any help from her whilst she prepared the meal. Hilary and Katie began chatting with each other about the odd little village and the strange parade of animals wandering the streets.

"I fink iz a goat… iz a goat." Katie peered out the window at a curly-haired creature with a pointy snout and horselike teeth chewing on the leg of a chair just outside the window. The goat looked up at the girls and let out a loud, shrill scream. Both girls laughed.

"Oi! Hils! Look at that!" Katie said, pointing and jumping up and down several times in excitement. One of the huge, hairy, oxen-like creatures was being led back into the town from the fields. The man leading it was carrying what resembled a horseshoe that the beast had apparently thrown. She surmised they were headed to the blacksmith to have it refitted.

The beast was taller than the man, and its snout reminded Hilary of her father's nose, which seemed to spread wider and become more porous with every passing year. The creature had a dozen rounded horns running down its spine, which perfectly parted its long mane down the middle of its back as though someone had flawlessly combed it that way.

Katie and Hilary stared silently as the beast disappeared into the stable.

"Oi, Hils," Katie whispered in a very serious tone. "I don't fink these folks are local."

Hilary nodded and cracked a smile. "Have you noticed," she said, "none of these people have a northern accent? They sound more like Mina."

Katie nodded. "Like I said, not local."

Theresa had been explaining a brief version of their adventures to Chloe when Moiré called out from the other room with panic in her voice. "Mamaí! An féidir leat teacht i anseo ar an bpointe boise?"

Chloe, Theresa, and Katie quickly hurried into the bedroom, fearing that Mina had taken a turn for the worse.

Hilary continued watching something through the window that had just caught her eye.

"*Cad is leanbh mícheart ann?*" Chloe asked with concern in her voice.

Moiré had rolled up Mina's sleeves and trousers to cool her fevered body with the wet cloth. She pointed to the fish scales that had appeared on Mina's legs.

"My God!" Chloe stumbled backward several steps, covering her mouth and nose with her hands.

"Actually, she's 'alf elf an 'alf muhmaid!" Katie finally proclaimed.

"It's her! *The Hidden Child!* I never dreamed I'd live to see this day!" Chloe cried out in disbelief, tears filling her eyes.

"You know of the prophecy?" Theresa ignored Katie. She wondered just how much the old woman knew of her world, or perhaps if she herself and the townspeople might be descendants of Balynfirth.

"Yes, I do." The woman's voice quivered a bit. "Treena, what is your part in this?"

"My father was an elder of the Aoileach people, and my mum… was Native American Indian." She wondered if Chloe would know of the prophecy concerning her as well.

"Daughter of Both Worlds. You're the Bridge. My God, I had no idea! It's coming to pass! It's actually happening now!" Chloe exclaimed, again holding her hands to her face in shock.

Chapter Eleven

Through the Window

MOIRÉ COULD CONTAIN herself no longer. *"An n-inseoidh duine éigin dom cad atá ar siúl anseo le do thoil? Cé hiad na daoine seo?"* She sounded frightened and confused.

Chloe gently put her hand on her daughter's shoulder. She had forgotten that the poor child didn't understand a word of English. Chloe began, *"Lad seo an-speisialta folks..."*

Suddenly Hilary called out from the other room. "Theresa, we have a problem!" With every word, Hilary's voice went higher.

Theresa, Chloe, and Katie hurried into the main room. Moiré followed, leaving the sleeping Mina on her bed.

Hilary was crouched now, peering just over the bottom of the window.

"Get down!" she warned them in a loud whisper as they approached the window.

A drunken man staggered across the town square, holding a nearly empty bottle of mead in his bandaged hand. With his other hand, he shoved a woman vendor out of his way and helped himself to some of the dried fruit on her stand. After a moment, he spat it on the ground and swore at her.

"Thomas…" Theresa felt her skin crawl at the sight of the man. She quickly pulled away from the window and fell back against the wall, looking very pale. She sank to her knees.

"*That's* the man who has been trying to kill you?" Chloe exclaimed in horror.

Theresa nodded, her eyes closed, her back against the wall.

Katie added, "Oh shit shite, shit shite, shit on a stick, shit shite…"

Theresa was motionless and silent for a long moment. Mina had said that in her death dream, Thomas was missing several fingers.

"What happened to his hand?" Theresa said.

Chloe replied in an almost apologetic tone. "He wandered into the village more than a week ago, nearly frozen. Flesh rot had set in. I'm sorry, Treena—Theresa. We didn't know what he was."

"*Tá an fear sin a Diabhail taobh istigh air,*" Moiré said, hushed but firm.

Theresa opened her eyes. "Yes, Moiré. He has the devil inside him. *Tá sé… an… Diabhail.*"

"We must hide you and get him out of here," Chloe said. She turned her attention to Moiré. "*Tabhair liom an seanbhuidéal sin de mhóinéad mulled.*"

Moiré quickly searched the cupboard and returned with a very old dusty bottle.

Chloe pulled the cork from the bottle with her teeth and sampled a big glug. "Damn, that's good." She licked her lips and offered it to Theresa, who also sampled it with a nod.

Chloe then gathered her herbs, and after mixing and grinding up several large pinches, she poured the powder into the glass bottle of mead. "I was saving this bottle for a special occasion. I guess this is it. Is he still out there?" She replaced the cork and shook the mead vigorously.

"He just went into the large building on the left!" Hilary replied.

"Moiré," Chloe said, "*chomh tapa agus is féidir leat, é seo a thógáil agus é a chur sa scioból áit a gcodlaíonn sé agus rith ar ais anseo láithreach. Ná lig dó tú a fheiceáil!*"

Moiré hesitated for a moment, then nodded with fear in her eyes and crept to the door with the bottle.

"What she doing?" Katie asked.

"The man is a slave to drink. What I put in that bottle will make him sleep for more than a day," Chloe said. "We'll deal with him then."

"Please, Chloe, you're putting yourself and Moiré in grave danger! We should leave now!" Theresa said.

"No!" Chloe said firmly, wagging her bony finger in Theresa's face. "You refused to listen to me as a child, but you *will* listen to me now!" A fierceness filled Chloe's eyes.

Theresa froze and nodded.

"Go, baby, and be quick!" Chloe said in almost a whisper.

Moiré nodded and dashed out the door for the barn.

"He's coming back out!" Hilary announced several minutes later. Moiré still had not returned.

Thomas was staggering out the door, trying to grasp a chicken by the legs with his damaged hand. The bird, apparently his dinner to be, flapped its wings and squawked in horror as he stumbled back toward the barn.

12 Chapter Twelve

Old Mead and Chicken

MOIRÉ CAREFULLY PLACED the bottle of mead near the man's sleeping place. She arranged a bit of straw around it, making it appear to have been there a while but quite visible to him. She quietly hurried back toward the doorway, her heart racing from the adrenaline pumping through her veins, when a shadow appeared just outside the door. It was the man. Moiré was trapped.

Tom closed the door behind him and fixed his eyes on the wooden chopping block he had appropriated and the hatchet lodged in its centre, his dinner flapping its wings and squawking as it hung helplessly upside down in his iron grip.

As he moved toward the block, a sound nearby caught his attention, and his fierce eyes moved toward it. Distracted, Tom lost his grip on the bird, which had managed to free one of its legs. He tried to re-establish his hold, but the terrified bird sank its razor-sharp beak into Tom's palm, slicing through his flesh. White-hot pain surged up Tom's arm, making him release his prize. It scrambled away, wings beating frantically as it desperately sought refuge from its executioner.

"Come back here, you little bastard!" Tom staggered to recapture his prize, but the bird was nowhere to be seen. He stood motionless, listening for any sound that would reveal his dinner's location as his eyes scanned the barn for movement. Several minutes passed. Silence filled his ears.

"Bastard," Tom mumbled as he placed his bleeding hand to his mouth. "I will find you!"

He staggered toward his sleeping place, taking a moment to unbutton his trousers and relieve himself on one of the stalls. He left a trail of brown urine on the wood and a dribble down his own trousers and bandaged hand.

After a moment, he plopped down onto the pile of hay, angry and defeated.

He hated this place. He hated the people and the food. He even hated the odd-looking chickens that tasted gamey and seemed to be made of all dark meat, which he also hated.

Tom's thoughts of hate suddenly stopped as he raised an eyebrow at something his bloodshot eyes had just caught. Crawling on all fours, he grasped a bottle partially buried in the straw.

"Well, at least I have you!" he proclaimed in victory as he pulled the cork with his teeth and took a deep sniff of its contents. He pulled his head back slightly and stared into it. It smelled a bit different from the other bottles of mead—which he also hated.

Tom took a big glug of the liquid and wiped his mouth on his sleeve, setting the bottle between his legs. He let out an enormous belch and leaned back against the stall wall, closing his eyes.

He'd drunk nearly half the bottle when a sound from across the barn entered his ears and his eyes flashed open. The room seemed to be spinning. After another glug, he closed his eyes again.

Moiré held the bird tightly under her arm, gently stroking its head and neck feathers. From the position atop the loft where she and her friend hid, she couldn't see what the man was doing down below. She would wait a few more minutes before venturing back down in hopes that he would be unconscious from the tainted mead.

Her heart pounded in her chest as she listened for any sounds of the man. The stable loft was a place she and Yavin would often come after their daily chores were finished. They would giggle for hours, often chucking straw at each other and stuffing dried grass down each other's backs, leaving an itchy rash that neither could reach to scratch and that would keep them awake at night. She smiled at the memories.

The sound of paper wasps could be heard in the rafters above her as they were busily constructing their new nest. Yavin's father, Mitchell, had promised to have one of his men deal with it soon, before summer set in and they became a serious problem, probably on a cool evening when they were not as active.

Her thoughts were interrupted by the sound of wood creaking down below, near the stairs leading to the loft.

Moiré's heart raced, as she feared it might be the man, but no further sounds entered her ears, and her mind soon returned to her afternoons with Yavin.

She looked at the large sliding door at the end of the loft where the men would often throw the bales of hay down onto a cart below to feed the prax who worked so hard pulling ploughs and drawing the carts. She would often sneak them a boiled sweet from her mum's kitchen as a little treat. The prax loved them; she did too, almost as much as…

Suddenly an odour filled her nostrils, a horrible smell, the smell of vomit and the stench of the man. Moiré slowly turned her head back toward the wooden ladder behind her, and her eyes filled with tears.

"Hello, Poppet." His voice was deep and cruel, and his red eyes were fixed upon hers. "That's my dinner you're holding."

Mitchell unlocked the weapons cabinet with a small brass key, then handed a rifle to each of the three men with him. In silence, they loaded the weapons and headed toward the livery stable.

Chloe walked with them, Yavin at her side. She whispered something to the boy, who quickly departed to carry out her instructions.

Mitchell was a very kind and mild-mannered man who held a grudge against no one, but when roused to anger, he could be as fierce as a fire propelled by the wind on dry grass. At Chloe's urging, the council vote had been taken quickly and was unanimous based on the news she had brought them.

Mitchell's eyes were fixed upon the door as the men approached the stable.

Chloe had not seen that fire in his eyes in many a year. She had forgotten how stern his face could become.

They stopped just outside the door. The men looked each other in the eye as they prepared to enter. Mitchell scrubbed his ginger-and-grey-peppered goatee with his fingers and nodded to a man whose hand was on the latch of the stable door.

The door swung open, and the men entered quickly, the light from outside revealing the location of the man.

Mitchell instantly put Tom in his sights and let out a shrill whistle. "*Bog, agus is fear marbh tú,*" he said in a calm but firm tone.

Tom looked wretched and confused. He staggered back several steps as he attempted to focus his drugged eyes on the men below, nearly losing his balance and tumbling off the edge.

"What?" he mumbled, not understanding the old language.

Chloe entered the stable, folding her arms before Tom. "He said if you move, he will kill you."

"Mamaí!" Moiré cried out, her voice shaking in fear. She hurried over to the far edge of the loft, away from the man. She trembled, holding her bird tightly under her arm.

"*Fan ceart ansin,* a Moiré!" Mitchell commanded without flinching, his aim still dead centre of Tom's forehead. Moiré obeyed him, freezing in place.

"So," Tom said sarcastically, "someone in this wretched village *can* speak proper language!" He staggered a few more steps toward the edge of the loft. "The child stole my dinner! I was just taking back what was rightfully mine!" His speech was slurred.

"That hen is an egg hen and not for eating. Nothing in this village is yours, nothing—"

"Is this how you treat strangers? You kidnap them, cut off their fingers and toes, and then starve them? You're a sick lot, all of you!"

Yavin timidly entered the barn, carrying a burlap sack and a dried prax's bladder filled with water. He handed them to Chloe, who chucked them at the foot of the loft ladder. She motioned Yavin back out of the stable.

Mitchell never took his eyes off Tom as Chloe translated the vomit-covered man's words. He responded without blinking, "*Abair leis a fháil amach agus nach bhfuil teacht ar ais. Mura ndéanann sé, cuirfidh mé síos é san áit a seasann sé.*"

Chloe nodded and turned back to Tom. "Mr. Mitchell says get out and never come back, or he'll kill you where you stand."

"Oh, will he?" Tom laughed.

"I warn you, Thomas. Mitchell can take out a bird's-eye half a mile away with that rifle. I would heed his words if I were you."

Tom smiled an evil grin as he descended the ladder. "There is only one person in this world who calls me Thomas. She's here, isn't she?"

Chloe cringed inside, as she had unwittingly revealed that Theresa was known to her, but her face remained hard and without emotion. She pointed to the burlap sack at Tom's feet. "There is enough food and water to last you several days. Now get out!"

Tom smirked. "Yeah... She's here. Theresa, that old man, and those rotten kids. They're all here, aren't they? Is the child with the demon ears here too? You're in league with them, aren't you? That woman murdered my daughter. Did you know that? She murdered my brother Jimmy too in cold blood, set him alight and laughed about it! I deserve justice, and I *will* have it!"

Chloe stood silent. After a moment, Tom reached down, gathering the sack of food to himself, staring deep into Mitchell's eyes the entire time.

Tom reached for the water bladder.

"Leave it."

"Why?" Tom demanded.

"Because you're a lying bag of shite, that's why," Chloe said without hesitation.

Tom started walking toward her, his eyes fixed upon hers. The men sharpened their aim on his forehead.

Mitchell slightly lowered his rifle and spoke to Chloe. "*Abair leis, má thógann sé céim amháin eile, séidfidh mé a liathróidí as.*"

Chloe cracked a smile. "Mr Mitchell wants me to inform you that if you take one more step toward me, he will shoot off your balls."

Tom froze in his tracks, studying the eyes and the grip Mitchell had on his rifle. After a moment, he realised the man was dead serious. Tom smiled evilly. "Right then. I'll go, but I'm leaving because I choose to. Any friends of that woman's are my enemies... and I never forget my enemies." He headed to the stable door, burlap sack over his shoulder, then turned and sneered at Chloe. "Sod off, hag."

The men followed Tom out, their weapons still fixed on him. Moiré hurried down from the loft and clung to her mum, her arms tightly wrapped about her waist.

The men escorted Tom over four miles from the village, releasing him at the top of a hill leading to a valley below. The men rested and watched Tom descend the hill, then disappear at the far end of the valley, over the next hilltop.

By the time they returned to the village, the skies had become overcast and grey with a promise of heavy rain. A bitter wind swirled in the air as dark clouds rumbled above. A storm was coming, the final storm.

Chapter Thirteen

New Friends

"I REALLY THINK we should go," Theresa said with a wary eye toward the window. "I've brought you enough trouble."

Chloe continued the meal preparations without looking up. "You have indeed, Theresa. But you and these children are not going anywhere until you've had a proper meal and a good night's sleep. Mina will need more attention from me as well. She's not out of the woods yet, and the two of you are far too important to let you just run off without a plan."

A loud clap of thunder punctuated Chloe's words, convincing Theresa to stay the night. She quietly seated herself at the table, relighting her pipe. Chloe was right. She and the children, especially Mina, would not get very far in their condition nor in the rain that had just begun.

"A plan?" Theresa asked.

"Yes. We need to talk about where you go from here."

"I guess I'm not quite sure now."

"That's why we need a plan. We'll talk about it on the morrow, Theresa."

"I don't suppose there is a telephone or telegraph here I might use?"

Chloe shook her head. "There is a town about nine miles or so to the east that has those machines and a road with those motorcar things. That would be your best option. You will have to pass through Black Forest to get there though."

Lightning flashed outside, spilling white light into the small house. Thunder sounded again seconds later with a loud *snap!* and rumbled in the faraway distance.

Mina suddenly cried out from the other room, "Mum? Mummy?"

Theresa, Chloe, Katie, and Hilary rushed to the room to find Mina sitting upright on the bed, drenched in sweat. Moiré, still at Mina's bedside, looked concerned.

"Mum?" Mina said with fear in her eyes, looking at the strange surroundings in confusion.

"I'm here, Mina! I'm here!"

Katie and Hilary looked at each other.

Katie raised an eyebrow and whispered, "Mum? I'm here!" to Hilary, mocking Mina's accent and then Theresa's.

Hilary let out a sigh with both eyebrows raised high.

Theresa took Moiré's place and felt Mina's forehead. To her astonishment, the fever had broken. She looked to Chloe for confirmation, and the old woman placed the back of her hand on Mina's forehead. After a moment, Chloe nodded to herself, turned, and left the room to gather her medicinal herbs.

"How are you feeling?" Theresa caressed the child's brow.

Mina didn't answer for a moment. A look of surprise came over her face as she stared into Theresa's eyes. She felt her ears, and after removing the cotton wads, now brown and sticky, she spoke. "I can… I can hear you. Well, a bit. Your words sound… mushy, but I can hear the sounds."

Theresa smiled as though a great burden had been lifted from her shoulders.

"I can hear myself too. I'd forgot what I sounded like, but it's my voice all right. I know it's mine because I've been hearing it all my life!"

As Theresa and Mina embraced, Chloe returned and made a fresh poultice, smellier than the last.

Lightning flashed again outside, followed by snapping thunder as the sky opened up. Mina shook in fear at the sight and sound of the dark omen. Theresa, knowing her thoughts, held her close.

"We won't go back to the cabin, Mina. We won't go anywhere near that place. In the morning we're going in a different direction to a town where we can get help. You don't need to be afraid. I'll protect you." Mina cried silently in Theresa's arms.

Chloe turned to Moiré, who was still feeling the trauma from the earlier scene in the stable. "Moiré, *cuimhnigh ar an dinnéar, mar sin ní scórálann sé. Beimid in éineacht leat i gceann cúpla nóiméad.*"

Moiré gritted her teeth and left the room silently, her eyes meeting both Hilary's and Katie's. All three girls seemed to be feeling the same emotions, left out and taken for granted.

"Katie, Hils, why don't you both help Moiré?" Theresa said without looking up.

"Help her what? We don't speak the same language!" Katie said, a hint of anger in her voice.

"Please, Katie. You can set the table!" Theresa replied, sensing the hurt in Katie's voice.

"Right... *Mum*," Katie said as she and Hilary left the room in a huff.

"Theresa, those two girls' noses are a bit out of joint." Chloe repacked the gauze into Mina's ears. "The elf calls you Mum. I think they are a bit jealous."

"Moiré didn't look too happy herself," Theresa said.

Chloe nodded. "I'll explain it to her. She'll understand."

Theresa helped Mina to the dinner table as she was still woozy. "What is this?" She pointed to her meal with her fork. "It's... familiar to me. It reminds me of haggis."

"Tebbin. I used to make it for you when you were staying with me. It was your favourite... before you killed my toilet!" Chloe replied, chuckling.

Moiré was feeling more left out than ever. She rested her chin on her hand, her eyes fixed on her meal, not understanding any of the past day's happenings nor the conversations taking place at the dinner table.

Mina took notice of the downcast girl seated next to Chloe and said, "Hello?" as Chloe disclosed the ingredients of the tebbin, prax organs and fermented root vegetables that neither Katie nor Hilary had ever heard of or cared to hear about… or eat again.

"Hello?" Mina said again to Moiré, who seemed to be in a fixed trance, repeatedly stabbing one of the grey root vegetables in her wooden bowl with her fork and leaving little rows of three all along the length of the root.

"She doesn't understand your language, child." Chloe instantly switched topics from prax intestines, testicles, and brains to Mina, who seemed hurt by the lack of Moiré's response.

Chloe turned to Moiré. *"Moiré, tá an elf ag caint leat. An féidir leat a rá Dia duit?"*

Moiré looked over to her mum and then toward Mina. *"Dia duit elf,"* she mumbled, refocusing her blank gaze at her food.

Mina crooked her head slightly and replied, *"Dia duit Moiré. Labhraíonn tú an tseanteanga. Go raibh maith agat as aire a thabhairt dom inniu. Tá a fhios agam nach bhfuil aithne agat orm, ach is mór agam gach a rinne tú. Is anam cineálta tú. Go raibh maith agat."*

Moiré raised her head, her bright blue eyes fixed on Mina. A smile slowly replaced her frown of displeasure. *"Tá fáilte romhat!"*

"What are they on about, T'reeza?" Katie asked.

"Mina thanked her for taking care of her, and Moiré said you're welcome."

"Mar sin, is elf tú?" Moiré asked Mina.

"Go páirteach… coillte-elf." Mina shrugged.

"Cén fáth a bhfuil tú go léir anseo?"

"Thug Theresa anseo mé. Bhí a fhios aici go bhféadfadh do mháthair cabhrú liom."

"I didn't quite get that." Theresa turned to Chloe.

"Moiré asked why you all came here. Mina said for us to care for her."

Theresa and Chloe exchanged smiles as the two girls seemed to hit it off. Soon they were giggling and sharing stories about themselves.

Katie and Hilary sat, quiet and motionless, as the others chatted together in the strange language. Even Theresa could now keep up with much of what sounded like gibberish to Katie and Hilary. Hils realised what Moiré must have been feeling in not being able to understand their language. Katie, on the other hand, was looking rather ill. The tebbin, and all the details of the meal's contents, had got the best of her.

Suddenly Katie jumped up from the table and bolted for the front door. The odd design of the door latch flummoxed her, and before she could pull the door open, her meal came back up, spraying the door and floor before her. Katie, looking quite pale, crumpled into a pile, moaning and holding her stomach. As Theresa and Chloe rushed to her, Katie cast her eyes down in embarrassment. "I don't fink I'll be eating tebbin stew again… Argh!"

Chloe did her best to provide the visitors a comfortable place to sleep, piling the floor with warm blankets and soft feather pillows.

Hilary, Katie, and Mina played several rounds of rock, paper, and scissors before snuggling down to sleep for the night. Moiré joined in the game, sharing rare laughter and smiles with the strangers, winning many of the rounds. She even offered up her own bed to Theresa, choosing to sleep next to the other children instead.

As Chloe and Theresa chatted at the table, the girls shared their stories with Moiré. It took a bit more time as Mina had to translate, but a bond of friendship grew between them. Moiré shared about her own life, losing her parents at a young age and Chloe taking her in as her own.

The four girls even taught each other some words and phrases of their own language, though Moiré struggled with Katie's thick accent, thinking it another language altogether. Hilary and Mina made sport of it, and even Moiré would giggle when Hilary or Mina had to ask Katie to repeat herself. Eventually the children fell asleep.

After a bowl of pipe weed, Theresa retired for the night. She found the bed quite small and lumpy, and her long legs hung over the edge as she lay awake, planning out the next day, determined to avoid the final confrontation with Thomas. She knew he would be back. She had to stay two steps ahead of him to protect Mina and the rest of the children. She must be ready for anything.

14 Chapter Fourteen

Hilary's Epiphany

HILARY AWOKE TO the sound of drizzle outside. It was still raining. Her back ached from sleeping on the hard stone floor.

Chloe was preparing breakfast on the peat-burning stove, a large rectangular metal box with a single door at the end that doubled as the winter heat source. Mina sat on the countertop nearby, her legs wiggling to and fro. She waved at Hilary, but Hils only replied with a grunt.

The smell of meat and eggs filled her nostrils as she shuffled into the loo, pulling the burlap curtain behind her.

She thought of the books she had read about America and how the skies were always blue and cloudless. She had had enough of this rainy, depressing country. She longed to move to California, where cowboys and Indians still ran wild, often having shootouts in the dusty streets, or perhaps a place called Florida, though she feared those monsters called crookodiles that were rumoured to crawl under locked doors at night and steal children from their beds. The wild beasts would then take the children back to their water caves and eat them alive, one piece at a time.

But Hilary reasoned that by the time the war was over and she could sail, or perhaps fly, to America, she would be old enough to fend off those crookodiles, and after all, after everything she had been through, she wasn't afraid of anything anymore… especially a beast that she could make into luggage.

On the other side of the burlap curtain, Hilary heard conversations and morning greetings as the others awakened and made their way to the table.

Katie was tickling Mina's feet as she wriggled and giggled and hiccupped from the countertop. Theresa shooed Katie away, and Katie protested and humphed over her spoilt fun. Moiré was setting the table and engaged the still-hiccupping Mina in conversation.

Hilary smiled at the sounds on the other side of the curtain. They were all a strange lot, but they were her family now. She loved them, and they loved her as well. She had a family!

Then the word came… breakfast was ready.

Hilary turned her thoughts to the strange toilet. The toilets at the *Wait* were just a series of wooden seats that opened to a long drop several stories below. With those toilets, they simply scattered a handful of some type of granules from a bowl next to them onto the waste, and it was composted to nothing by their next use. This, however, was quite different. Chloe had shown her how to use it the day before, but it was ever so complicated.

Hilary was still quite groggy, but she remembered that after using the handmade bog roll, she was to pour a bit of water into the bowl from the tin bucket next to her and pull the lever upward after unlatching it from its metal cradle. This would dump the waste into an enclosed metal trough, which was outside and on wheels. They would then empty this larger container every few days.

With her business finished, Hilary joined the rest of her family for breakfast.

15 Chapter Fifteen

Family

AS HILARY TOOK her seat, Chloe spoke. "Mr Mitchell was by a bit ago."

"Wicky? What did he want?" Theresa smiled.

"He has a proposition for you! He suggests you write a letter, and his best rider will take it to town and have it sent to the people you need help from using that teglagraf machine."

"Telegraph," Katie said with a full mouth, accidentally spewing a bite of egg across the table. "Sorry." She popped it back into her mouth with a silly grin.

Theresa rolled her eyes in embarrassment.

Chloe continued, "Day after tomorrow, he will escort you through the forest on foot to town where hopefully your friends will be waiting to help you finish this journey."

"This was his idea?" Theresa asked.

Chloe nodded with a smile. "He remembers you."

Theresa sat silently for a moment, deep in thought. She liked Mitchell and his kind demeanour but only vaguely remembered him from all those years ago.

The single memory she had of Mitchell was of a boy about her age who quietly fancied her but was too shy to even come within twenty feet. His face would become beet red every time her eyes caught his, and he'd quickly turn away and whistle some silly tune, his eyes darting about, hoping she hadn't noticed his obvious attraction to her. Theresa had never seen him without a hat.

"All right. I'll prepare the letters straightaway after breakfast. Thank you!"

"So... We're all going to go to Mina's world?" Hilary queried.

"Uh... no," Theresa replied.

"You just agreed to help Mina finish her journey."

"This journey *is* finished," Theresa said flatly, her eyes flashing momentarily to Mina, now sitting motionless and silent.

"Oi!" Katie said angrily. "So you're just going to dump us all back wif Medlock? Iz not 'appening! We go togevah!"

Hilary sat quietly next to Katie, nodding. "We're family now," she said. "Family sticks together."

"Yeah. Tha's right. We're family now!" Katie proclaimed dramatically with a nod.

Theresa sat stunned for a moment, a lump forming in her throat and tears welling up in her eyes. *Family.* She hadn't heard or used that word in many years. She understood its meaning but couldn't remember how it felt. A feeling of panic rose up within her—and the desire to run.

"Look, I care a great deal about you... all of you. Please believe me when I say that. But this nightmare needs to end. We have all experienced some really horrible things over the past few weeks... or months. I'm not even sure how long it's been anymore. Tad is dead, and we are very fortunate to still be alive after everything that has happened to us. This isn't my life. I didn't sign up for this. I want to go home. I promise you, all of you, that we will find a way to spend a lot of time together, but this isn't my life. I want my life back."

"Oh, so we're an 'orrible nightmare, and you'll find a way to spend lots of time wif us in Cannich whilst you're in London. What a crock of sh—" Katie's words blistered Theresa's promise.

"That's not what I meant, Katie. I just—"

"So you don't want us? Eh?" Hilary demanded.

Mina raised her head and looked into Theresa's eyes as the woman spoke.

"No. I'm sorry."

Dank silence descended into the house. Everything felt grey and cold to its occupants.

Theresa quietly ate her breakfast though it now tasted like sand. The children sat unmoving, their eyes fixed downward. Theresa ignored Chloe's stare, which was drilling a hole through her soul, and Hilary's word *family* echoed over and over in her head.

Whilst Moiré didn't understand the words that had been spoken, she well understood the body language that had so suddenly changed. She could feel the energy of the room shift, and she knew Theresa had just rejected the children.

Outwardly, Theresa remained unmoved, though she felt a great storm raging within. She quietly lit her pipe with trembling hands and began writing the two letters, one to Melody and one to Medlock, on the handmade parchment that Chloe had set next to her breakfast plate earlier. The others sat in silence as she penned the long letters; the only sounds were the scratching sound of the quill on paper and their own heartbeats. Theresa folded the letters and handed them to Chloe.

Chloe reluctantly took them, set them on the table, and rested her hand upon them. She tapped the letters in rhythm with her crooked fingers before finally turning her attention to Moiré.

"Moiré, cén fáth nach dtógann tú do chairde nua chun bualadh le Yavin? Is dócha go bhfuil sé thall sa Teach Mór, ag cabhrú le hullmhú don chruinniú anocht. Tabharfaidh sé rud éigin le déanamh agat go léir inniu…"

Moiré nodded, casting a look of resentment toward Theresa. She motioned for the girls to follow her. They quietly stood, leaving much of their uneaten breakfast behind.

Chapter Sixteen

Hidden Child

CHLOE POURED HERSELF and Theresa another cup of tea, then sat in silence.

Theresa rubbed her forehead whilst replaying the horrible choice of words she had just used and, after a long moment, looked up to meet Chloe's eyes. "I don't think they understood what I was trying to say."

Chloe sipped on her tea, which was cradled in both hands, her wrinkled elbows propped upon the wooden table. "They understood."

"It's just too dangerous for them. I'm concerned that something could happen. Thomas has it out for me and could come back. And the children…" Theresa faltered as she began replaying her last words to them again in her mind.

"This is because of your daughter?" Chloe asked calmly.

"What? What does that have to do with this?" Theresa fired back angrily, remembering a similar confrontation she had had with Melody before leaving to search for the runaway Mina. "This is a totally different situation! It's the children's welfare I'm thinking about!" Theresa stared deep into her teacup with unfocused eyes. "This has nothing to do with Mina. I mean Lucy."

Chloe slurped her tea yet again. "I see."

The two women sat in silence for several moments. The only sound was that of a distant prax braying in the barn.

"Theresa," Chloe said. "Did you know that much of our lives are decided at the kitchen table?"

"Sorry?" Theresa was lost in her own thoughts and the empty feeling now growing in her heart.

"Much, if not *most*, of who we are, who we become, what we believe, and the choices we make that impact our lives, is decided at the kitchen table."

"What's your point, Chloe?" Theresa rubbed her forehead again in irritation.

"At this table, in an instant, you decided the fate of those three children with no real thought or consideration for them or their needs. You just played God."

Anger flashed in Theresa's eyes. "I just *told you* that my concern is only for them!"

Chloe nodded insincerely. "Yes, you did tell me that. And what of Mina?"

"What about her?"

"She doesn't have much time left. I thought you might want to make her last days good days and take her home. You are the only one who can open the door for her. She has the key, but only you can turn it. You are the bridge between both worlds."

A look of shock came over Theresa's face. "I'm NOT playing God! And I'm not some bridge! I'm just an ordinary woman who wants to go home! And what do you mean, she hasn't much time left? Has she been telling you about her dreams?"

Chloe raised her eyebrows. "Dreams? Mina has *sight?*" Chloe set her cup down on the table with a clunk. "Of course she does. She's seeing things before they happen, isn't she? Is she dreaming about her own death?"

Theresa nodded. "Not for a while. She's had a recurring dream that Thomas kills her and she dies in my arms. But it's been a while since she had that dream. It happens at that cabin—and we are NOT going anywhere near that place! She's safe, Chloe. They are all safe! I've done my job. I can go home now."

Chloe sighed. "Theresa, Mina is dying. The Hidden Child is a cross between mer and elf folk. They were not meant to procreate. They are two different species. She is the only offspring of mer and elf... ever. She has no kinsman of her own. She is not mer-kind, and she is not elf-kind. She is alone in both worlds. Look at how small and frail she is. Look at how prone to illness she is. She wasn't meant to live very long. It won't matter if Thomas finds her or not. She's dying."

"You're saying she's destined to die, and that's why I don't want to keep her with me, because of how Lucy's death affected me? Because I couldn't bear to lose another..." Theresa's voice faltered.

Chloe nodded. "That's exactly what I'm saying."

Theresa slammed her cup to the table and stood up in anger. "You don't know what you're talking about! I have protected and saved that child's life more times than I can count! Who are you to question my motives? That dream is *not* going to happen, because I am getting as far away from here and that psychopath as I can get! I *am* protecting her! How dare you question my commitment to her... or any of the girls, for that matter! I've risked my life for them more times than any mother would ever have! Once I'm gone, they will all be safe."

Chloe shook her head sadly. "You don't understand. She's the Hidden Child."

"So?" Theresa said, fear rising in her voice.

"Think. What does hidden mean?"

"Um... She was hidden here in this world, I guess."

Chloe closed her eyes, again shaking her head. "Remember the old language, Theresa. It means unloved sacrifice. How is it you don't even know the language and prophecies of your own people? That is a very old prophecy."

Theresa chewed on her bottom lip as she slowly reseated herself.

Chloe continued, "Her purpose, as the Hidden, is to save Balynfirth and its peoples. She was not meant to have a life of her own. She is the fulfilment of the prophecy. Both of you are. We can't choose our destinies, but we can choose how we face them when the time comes. When Mina was born, the prophecy said that the Hidden and her protector-mother would be needed to save Balynfirth from darkness. So it is told, when Mina's protector arrived, they would face the forces of evil together. You are her protector-mother, Theresa. You are Mina's other half in this story."

"I'm not her mother, Chloe."

Chloe tucked her long grey hair behind her ear, revealing pointed ears. "I'm part elf-kind and part Aoileach. I am one hundred and sixty-one years old. I've borne children, many of them. She can't. She is like a mule, part donkey, part horse, unable to procreate. Elf-kind and man-kind can mate and even procreate. Elf-kind and mer cannot. Yet somehow they did—in fulfilment of the prophecy. She is the Hidden. The universe designed it that way for a reason. Mina will never have children. She cannot. She will never grow up. She wasn't meant to. She will have passed from this world long before she can ever become a woman. She is the Unloved Sacrifice. She was rejected by the mer and rejected by the woods elves. She has never been loved, not even by her own mother, and it's only a mother's love—your love—that can save her. And now you have rejected her."

"How can you possibly know all this, Chloe?"

"I was there when the prophecy was given many, many years ago."

Anger flashed in Theresa's eyes at Chloe's words. "Why can't she have a life of her own? Why can't she grow up, marry, and have children? Why is that little girl condemned to die before her time? This makes no sense! It's just folklore that has been passed down and distorted over the years. It's rubbish. I'm *not* her mother."

Chloe stared deep into her eyes. "I can clearly see that now. So can she."

The sound of the door latch rattling broke the uncomfortable tension, and Mina quietly entered, looking very grim.

"What's wrong, Mina?" Theresa asked as the little girl approached, contorting her face into unpleasant expressions.

"I swallowed a bug."

"Here, take a sip of tea. It'll get the taste out of your mouth."

Mina took a big glug of the now-lukewarm tea. "Thank you," she said politely, unwilling to give Theresa eye contact. "Um… I need the fluty thing."

"What fluty thing?" Theresa asked.

"The one in your bag."

"You went through my bag?"

"No! I dreamed about it, and we are going to play some music together—me and Hilary and Katie and Moiré and, um… Yavin. Some other people too, but I forget their names, don't you know."

"You're dreaming again?"

"Yes," she replied rather aloofly.

"Did you dream about… well, you know?" Theresa probed.

Mina nodded.

"I won't let that happen, Mina. Bring me the bag."

After rummaging through her satchel, Theresa pulled out the elven windpipe and handed it to Mina.

"May I see it?" Chloe asked.

"Shoh." Mina imitated Katie's accent as she passed the weapon to Chloe.

Chloe's eyes grew wide as she held and turned it carefully, as though it was some rare and valuable jewel. "This is very powerful, but you *know* that, don't you?"

Mina nodded. "I promise I'll be careful and just play music on it. I promise."

Chloe smiled and handed the flute to the child, who politely thanked her and hurried back out the door without giving eye contact to Theresa.

Chloe turned to Theresa. "The children, including Mina, are welcome to stay here with us. We can give them a home, and they will be well cared for, and they won't have to grow up in an orphanage alone or be around that war of yours," she said with a sigh. "We will be their family. You can go back to your… *life*… alone."

Theresa sat silent for a moment and then nodded.

Chloe rose from the table and gathered two new sheets of parchment, the quill, and the vial of ink. Theresa rewrote the letters to Medlock and Melody.

A knock on the door sounded as Theresa signed the last letter. It was Ned, the rider. She handed both letters to him, thanked him, and he was off.

Mina walked back toward the Big House to rejoin her friends whilst humming a little tune. She carefully looked over the strange musical instrument, turning it and studying it from every angle as a big gust of wind rustled the trees in the distance that were now crowned with young leaves. Mina stood motionless, listening to the sound of the trees and mostly the silent spaces between the gusts of wind.

Mina slowly turned in a circle, her eyes closed as the trees spoke to her. After a moment, she opened her eyes. They filled with tears as she accepted the instructions.

Chapter Seventeen

Reflection and Tiny Faces

WITH THE GIRLS busying themselves with new friends, Theresa had the opportunity to spend some time alone.

She enjoyed the last of her pipe weed as she walked about the village, reacquainting herself with its surroundings. For so many years, she had blocked this place and all her childhood memories from her mind. As her dormant brain cells were reactivated by the sights and sounds, she revisited many splintered memories of not only this village but of her own family and childhood. Her memories were mostly flashes, images, and emotions, but more and more of the pieces were coming together like the assembling of a jigsaw puzzle.

Several boys were laughing and showing off to each other as they had a wager as to who could do the most pull-ups whilst hanging from a tree branch by their hands. One boy was Yavin, Mitchell's only son. He looked exactly like Mitchell had as a child. He smiled at her as she walked by, his face slightly turning pink as Mitchell's would when she caught him staring at her.

Mitchell approached the boys from the opposite side of the village. His eyes met Theresa's.

Theresa overheard him talking to Yavin. "Boy! What do you have to do if you want a washboard stomach?" Yavin quickly replied to the question he had heard many times before. "Lift them high and hold them straight!"

Theresa turned to see the boy lifting his legs straight out and holding his abdominal muscles tight for as long as he could. She smiled at Mitchell, who was obviously showing off his parenting skills for her.

Her thoughts turned to Melody and then the three children. Despite all the trauma and turmoil of the past few months, she felt more alive now than she had her entire life. Would that feeling change when she went home... alone?

She stood deep in thought at the edge of the village, looking out toward the Caledonian Forest, or the Black Forest, as these villagers referred to it. Theresa studied the dark storm clouds gathering above the trees and the fog silently filling in the gaps with its grey mist. A storm was gathering.

Out of the corner of her eye, Theresa sensed something moving below her. Several somethings...

Brought back to the present, she eyed the wild orchids at her feet. They differed greatly from her orchids back home, more like a dense groundcover, and seemed to have a consciousness about them. Theresa felt as if they were studying her. They covered the landscape as far as she could see, becoming blacker as they approached the forest.

Theresa stooped down to inspect the flowers, gently lifting a bloom upward. A chill ran down her neck. It had a face! A real face! The face had long oval eyes, a Jimmy Durante nose, two tiny holes for nostrils, and a lipless mouth. It smiled up at her, emanating a calming energy that flooded Theresa's body and soul. As she looked more carefully, she noticed that all the orchids had similar faces.

Some of them slept soundly, and some smiled toward the vanishing sun, receiving the last of the Scottish morning sunshine and warmth with joy. A few looked at her with great curiosity, and one even let out a little yawn.

Theresa listened intently; she could hear the tiny snoring of the sleeping harbingers.

These flowers were from the other world. Somehow they were now in this place, either by proximity to the portal or having been brought here like the prax beasts, odd chickens, fruits, and vegetables by visiting woods elves and Aoileach.

Theresa smiled at the face before her. She gently caressed its little cheek with her fingers. It smiled brightly back at her. She carefully lowered it back down. Theresa stood and slowly backed away so as not to step on any of them.

Theresa felt a presence behind her. Without turning, she spoke. "*Dia duit*, Wicky."

The man stood by her side without a word. Theresa looked over to see Mitchell's face becoming flushed like when he was a child. She smiled.

"You remember me?" he asked shyly, looking at the darkening forest before them.

"Yes, Wicky, I remember you."

"I never thought I would see you again," he said, almost in a whisper.

"Well, you were wrong, weren't you?" she said with feigned cheerfulness.

Mitchell looked to the ground, a smile creeping over his face. "Indeed."

"So," Theresa said, "you have a family now."

The smile faded from his face. "I have a son, Yavin. You'll get to meet him proper tonight."

"And your wife?" Theresa asked, feeling awkward at his response.

"Aggie passed three winters ago. It was a sudden illness." His voice cracked slightly.

"I'm so sorry. I didn't know." She regretted bringing up the subject.

Mitchell rubbed his goatee, finally looking Theresa in the eye. "Ned is my best rider. He should be on his way back by now, hopefully with a response from your friend... Melody? Did I pronounce her name correctly?"

Theresa smiled. "Yes, you did."

They looked into each other's eyes in silence.

"You know, I still can't tell what colour your eyes are. Sort of blue green... maybe a deep aqua. I'm not sure," she said.

He smiled shyly, turning beet red again. Theresa gently caressed his cheek.

"I'll see you tonight." With that, he turned and sauntered back toward the village, whistling a silly tune.

Theresa watched him for a moment before returning her gaze to the forest. Just the sight of the dark, ominous place left Theresa feeling chilled inside. Tomorrow she would have to go through it on her way home, alone.

Chapter Eighteen

Life Crumbling Around

A SINGLE CANDLE in Melody and Theresa's home flickered as the wind from outside found its way in through a gap in the nearby window. It toyed with the flame on the kitchen table.

Over the top of her spectacles, Melody read the telegram she had received that afternoon. She had to keep rereading the same sections over and over as the latest bombing was disrupting her concentration. On one hand, she felt a wave of relief wash over her knowing that Theresa and Mina were safe. On the other, the stress she had been under the past month had been more than she could bear alone.

Another area hospital had been completely levelled by the Germans in a night raid nearly a month ago. The doctors and nurses that had survived had been reassigned to the hospital where Melody worked. She had been given the sack, not because of her nursing skills, which rivalled those of many of the practicing doctors, but because she was not a citizen of the UK and they felt it inappropriate to keep her at the expense of an out-of-work Brit.

Because of the loss of her job, she was more than a month past due for rent and the landlord was threatening them with dispossession.

Tomorrow was the deadline he had given her to have the money paid in full, or he vowed to change the locks and set the wheels in motion to have her deported back to the US.

The house suddenly shook, bringing her back into the present moment. Melody lifted her eyes to the dust filtering down from the growing cracks in the ceiling. In the dim candlelight, the dust glittered faintly all around her, accentuating the loneliness she felt within.

The almost nonstop barrage of bombing had taken its toll on her. For more than a week, air-raid sirens had been shattering the nighttime silence relentlessly so that Melody scarcely slept at all. Now, in the morning, she would have to trek across the country to retrieve Theresa with little more than five pounds to her name. After all Theresa had been through, confessing that not only were they losing their home but that she might be deported back to the US was more than Melody wanted to burden her friend with.

Tears trickled down her cheeks as the nonstop bombs sounded around her, tormenting her ears and mind. She dropped her head into her hands.

Suddenly the house rocked violently. Sections of plaster from the ceiling crashed down upon the kitchen table, filling the room with dust and debris. The hair on the back of her neck stood on end, and instinctively she felt the urge to run.

She snatched the telegram and stuffed it into her blouse as she bolted for the front door. Another horrible sound blasted, and Melody felt the walls and ceiling around her being lifted from the ground as the house collapsed around her.

Chapter Nineteen

The Big House

THERESA AND CHLOE approached the Big House, each carrying a hot potato casserole. They were running a bit late as they had spent a great deal of time weeding through the bin in the root cellar, searching for good potatoes. Theresa had never seen purple potatoes before, or if she had, she had forgotten. Blight on the previous year's crop had left many of them diseased and rotting.

The heat from the hot dish warmed Theresa's hands, and the Celtic music and dance had already begun. Another spring storm was moving in from the Black Forest. In front of the storm, strong winds and a cold chill filled the air. The trees swayed in the wind, rustling their new crown of leaves, and they seemed to be trying to warn her about something.

Theresa stopped for a moment and listened to the strange voices. They had always been there, but she had never truly listened before. Her mind emptied of all thought, and she felt herself enveloped in the strange connection with the trees. Whispered stories and warnings filled her mind, not in words but in feelings.

"Theresa?" Chloe said, snapping her out of the trance.

She realised she had come to a complete stop, perhaps for a full minute, whilst her soul had permitted—for the first time in many years—the voices of the trees to speak to her.

"Sorry." She blinked several times, shivering as they reached the Big House.

The Big House was the only building in town, except the livery stable, that was constructed entirely from wood. The villagers' homes were all built from rock, thatch, and peat. Theresa wondered if there was some remaining reverence for the ancient trees that limited the use of wood in this strange place.

Her eyes searched for the three girls in the crowded building. It was indeed a big house, as all the people of the village were now under its roof, laughing and dancing in joyful fashion.

Near the centre of the room was a stage, built several feet above the crowd. A band of local musicians played the most delightful music she had ever heard. It certainly had Celtic influence at its core but was somehow different.

She studied the ancient musical instruments: mandolins, kanoun, hurdy-gurdy, uilleann pipes, bodhran, oud, bouzouki, two fiddles, harp, lyra, tabla, unique percussion instruments of different sizes, hammer dulcimer, and even a cello. Several of the instruments she didn't recognise, though the sounds they created were familiar to her from long ago.

Theresa spotted Katie. She was playing a mandolin. She had no idea that Katie was a musician, and from what she could hear, a very good one.

She wished she was onstage with them and her flute.

The villagers were dancing in an intricately choreographed manner. Two circles of people surrounded the stage; the smaller circle was moving clockwise as they locked arms and moved their feet in perfect synchronisation to the music.

The outer circle was much the same, though dancing counterclockwise, with more emphasis on turns and switching partners every few seconds. The outer circle clapped their hands at precise moments in rhythm of the music as the inner circle stomped their heels on the offbeat.

Theresa's mind flashed back to her childhood, a time she was dancing around a bonfire in the forest. She remembered her father and uncle watching her from the old log as she danced in delight, the light from the fire flickering on their faces. It was very similar music, the dance nearly identical. Instinctively, she knew every step and could anticipate when the outer circle would turn and clap. She knew this dance. She had danced this dance.

A particular dancer in a gypsy skirt and black boots caught her eye. It was Mina. Her mind travelled back even further as she watched the girl and her unique style. She had seen her dance before… long, long ago. Theresa remembered sitting on her mother's lap, Miramanee's lap; she was only about three. She had climbed down and done her own little dance as she watched the young girl, trying to imitate her moves. After a moment, the young girl came over to her, took her hands, and began dancing with her.

Theresa now remembered the girl's face. Mina's face. She was the same girl who was dancing before her now…

"Oh. My. God," Theresa mumbled aloud.

Chloe elbowed Theresa in the ribs, again bringing her back to the present, and motioned with her head and a smile to follow over to the banquet table. The two women placed their casseroles on the remaining open spots for the feast that would soon begin. Theresa again turned her eyes to the dancing Mina.

Katie and Hilary had taken the news about staying in the village rather well. Mina sat quietly as Theresa had informed them earlier that day of her plans to return to England alone. The ability to play music with the villagers was the single selling point to Katie. She loved music. Being able to jam with the locals had helped her mood considerably as did knowing that she wouldn't have to face Medlock or her wooden paddle again.

Hilary had resigned herself to the decision but felt deeply hurt and saddened inside at Theresa's rejection. Mina showed little emotion, choosing rather to play music on the fluty thing.

Mitchell called everyone to the long banquet table. They clasped hands and looked to the sky as he offered thanks for the meal and a blessing for the seeds that were to be planted on the morrow.

The musicians, including Katie, were first in line at the table as they would soon return to the stage after the feast to entertain the villagers in dance and song.

Katie carefully avoided anything that might have prax meat in it or that smelled the least bit suspicious, sticking mostly to vegetables that she recognised. She took a large scoop of the purple potato casserole and a cautious sniff of what looked like fish next to it. Her upper lip curled at the smell as she muttered, "Parasitic glurp." Her attention turned to finding something more appealing, or at least edible, on the long table. She eyed a strange green gruel in a wooden bowl. Every few seconds, a thick gas bubble would float to the top, making a *blaft* sound. Katie grimaced. "Fermented grelb." She scanned the table with frantic eyes, her eyebrows contorting into odd shapes. "This food isn't local."

Farther down the line, she came across something that looked a bit like a gourd. Katie sniffed it. It smelled like bread but had a strange texture to it. It was yellow with green streaks running through it and rounded like a football but flat on the bottom, with five raised triangular ridges coming to a point at the top. She whacked the strange gourd with the back of her spoon, hoping that the sound would somehow reveal to her whether it would be edible. It had a hollowness to it. *What was it?*

Chloe had been watching with a smirk on her face as Katie picked her way down the table with little more than a blop of potato casserole and several green carrots on her plate.

As Katie whapped the strange-looking orb with her spoon, Chloe approached from behind. "It's breadfruit, Katie. Try it. It's quite good!"

"What's breadfroo?" Katie asked suspiciously.

Chloe smiled. "It grows like cabbage on the ground. Once it's ripe, it's harvested and dried. We soak it in salt water and herbs and bake it. Try it!"

"Iz hard as a rock. It'll break all me teeth!"

Chloe took a sharp serrated knife from the table and cut it in half.

The steaming bread-like scent filled Katie's nostrils. She breathed it in deeply. "Mmmn…"

"You eat the centre and leave the hard shell. Just don't eat the seeds. They'll grow in your stomach and out of your mouth!"

"What?" Katie exclaimed dramatically, suddenly visualising some strange plant with leaves growing out of her mouth and nostrils.

Chloe laughed, her wrinkled face scrunching tight. "I'm joking, Katie! Give it a go!"

Katie cautiously plucked a chunk of the strange food from the centre, taking a nibble. To her surprise, she found it quite delicious. It reminded her of the wheat rolls Miss Hatchett at Saint Austin's would make for holiday meals.

"You sure iz not a vegetable instead of a fruit?" Katie asked.

"You're very clever, Katie! It actually is a vegetable, but it's been called breadfruit for as long as I can remember."

Suddenly Chloe winced in pain, nearly falling forward onto the table.

"You ole right, Chloe?" Katie asked, concern filling her face.

"Oh, I'm fine, child. I'm fine." She said, searching for breath.

After a moment, Chloe smiled and led her to a few other dishes, pointing out what might seem more traditional to the girl. Soon Katie's plate was filled several layers deep in food, and she wore her big Katie grin as she found her new friends at a table nearby.

20 Chapter Twenty

The Old Song

T HERESA WATCHED AS the musicians returned to the stage, Katie amongst them. She realised that even though Katie scarcely understood a single word anyone said, they all spoke the universal language of music.

They played the "Song of Thanks" to begin, a lovely round. To Theresa's surprise, Katie sang a verse in English to the smiling villagers—Mina must have provided her a translation—before the round portion began.

Theresa sat at a table with Chloe, Hilary, and a very quiet Mina as she listened to Katie singing and playing the mandolin. Oddly, Katie's thick accent all but disappeared when she sang. She had a beautiful voice. Theresa felt very proud of her at this moment but also a bit ashamed that she hadn't known until now just how talented Katie was.

Soon the music became a joyful Celtic dance, Moiré leading the way with her fiddle. Some of the villagers returned to the floor to dance while others finished their meals and engaged in conversation. After nearly an hour, Mina joined the musicians on stage. Moiré took a moment to check her fiddle's tuning as Mina readied her flute.

Silence filled the room. By the reaction of the crowd, Theresa realised that this must be a special moment, something for which everyone had been waiting.

Moiré began playing the musical instrument with slow, sweeping movements. An energy filled the room that Theresa had never experienced before, which everyone could obviously feel. This was the climax of the evening. Theresa scarcely could believe her ears at the music that permeated every fibre of her being.

Mina joined with Moiré in perfect harmony with her elven flute, an eerie-sounding instrument. As the two girls played, all who heard became totally entranced by the music. Theresa found herself being emotionally pulled into the seductive sound as it reminded her of when Mina sang the "Siren's Song." She tried to resist it but couldn't. No one even blinked during the entire song, though tears streamed down their faces.

Theresa felt as though her soul had been touched, deeply and profoundly. This was the "Song of Loss," expressing respect and mourning for those lost to death in the past years. She thought of her uncle Tad.

The enveloping energy subsided though, leaving its mark permanently on everyone who had ears to hear. The crowd sat in silence for a long moment as the trance slowly dissolved.

Applause filled the room as the villagers looked to the sky with thoughts of their loved ones in their hearts. As the applause ended, Mina rushed down the stairs from the stage and grasped Theresa's hand. Startled, Theresa followed her up onto the stage.

Theresa could feel her face turning beet red as Mina gathered her elven flute. The rest of the band readied themselves.

"What… What are we doing, Mina?" Theresa stammered, feeling very on the spot.

"Will you sing the spirit guardian song that you sing at your house?" the little girl pleaded with big eyes. "You know, the kind of chanty song, the one that has no words? I taught it to the others, and Katie wrote some music for it. Will you sing it like you do at your home?"

"Spirit guardian? Mina," she whispered, "I can't remember all of it. I never could, just bits and pieces."

"You will!" Mina smiled as she moved away from centre stage and took up her flute.

Theresa felt very self-conscious. She had no idea that Mina had ever heard her singing that old chant. How could she have?

After an uncomfortable moment, with all eyes upon her, she gathered a wooden stool and seated herself amid the musicians. Katie whispered some instructions to Theresa as to the arrangement she had composed. Theresa nodded and cleared her throat.

"This is a song my mum taught me many years ago," she said to the crowd, forgetting to translate her words into the old language. "Her mum had taught it to her as well. It was a call to the spirits for help in time of need. She was a native American Indian from across the pond. I hope you like it."

Suddenly a rhythm began playing on a set of small percussion drums, taking Theresa by surprise. She looked at Katie for guidance as the rhythm repeated several times. Katie just smiled and showed her three fingers, then two, then one. On the next count, Katie pointed to her and mouthed the word *now*.

Theresa began singing the song so quietly that she couldn't even hear her own voice. It took a moment to synchronise with the tempo of Katie's arrangement and Mina's flute, but only a moment.

She raised the volume of her own voice and felt a chill crawl up her spine as the acoustics of the big room created an eerie but very pleasing rendition of the chant that she could never have imagined. Her voice seemed to echo almost a three-part harmony in the song that charged her soul. As she grew more confident, the sound became even more powerful.

The eerie chant echoed in the wooden timbers and reverberated around the room, creating an otherworldly feel. There were no words to it, but it didn't need any.

Theresa felt tears streaming down her face but didn't know why. A clap of thunder from the approaching storm above seemed perfectly timed as it punctuated the depth of the song, somehow giving it a more profound meaning.

Thomas stood amidst the black ground cover, looking for any sign of life. It had taken him many hours to circle back to this place after the men of the village had so rudely escorted him from it.

The air had become still, almost stagnant, the calm before the storm. Music in the distance filled his ears. He realised that every soul from the town was in the large wooden building, having some kind of party. Anger boiled in him; they were celebrating his banishment. Tom lit his torch, thinking he could end them all by simply barring the door and setting the peat-thatch roof alight.

He then recognised a voice; it was Theresa. She was singing that song. That horrible song he hated so much. He laughed aloud, feeling this was his lucky day. In the motionless air, Tom noticed the trees beginning to sway and the black flowers at his feet moving as Theresa's singing grew louder.

Lightning flashed above him followed by the roar of thunder. His eyes bloated as the leggy vines began wrapping themselves around his feet.

In a panic, Thomas tried to run, but the harbingers had a firm grasp and he fell face-first onto the ground, dropping his lit torch. The harbingers quickly smothered the fire. As he lay motionless, he realised that Theresa's song was now coming through the angry trees and the plants that had taken him captive. The sound was deafening.

Suddenly he felt himself moving. The plants were dragging him away from the village at breakneck speed toward the forest. Thomas clawed desperately at the ground as he was eaten by the blackness.

Mina quietly smiled to herself as she sensed that the trees and harbingers had completed their task… and just in time. If Theresa only knew what she had just done and how powerful the song she had just sung truly was.

As Theresa's singing ended, Katie's mandolin began a carefully directed rhythm, changing the song's direction but not its impact. Soon the other instruments joined in, blending the chant with an upbeat Celtic piece carefully composed by Katie. It was brilliant. The music concluded with a roar of applause.

Theresa gave a nod of appreciation to Mina and Katie. Her mother, Miramanee, and grandmother, Onawah, would have been very proud. If Moiré and Mina's "Song of Loss" was the highlight of the evening, this was the encore.

Chapter Twenty One

Going Home

THERESA LAY BACK onto the lumpy bed, with the spirit guardian song still running through her mind. This had been a wonderful evening. She didn't even mind the impending hangover from the three pints of mead that she was sure to have in the morning as she had earned it.

She could hear the girls chatting and giggling in the other room as she began drifting off to sleep.

The crackling thunderstorm had given way to a slow, steady rain, with lightning silently flashing every few seconds. The sound was music to her ears.

Theresa decided she would somehow convince Melody to return with her to this place to live. Chloe and several of the villagers had told her during the celebration that they would be most welcome and that they would even be provided with their own house. No more dealing with the ugly war, no more having to scrounge for mouldy food in the neighbours' dustbins whilst they were in their shelters during the German raids. A return to a simpler way of living.

She could stay close to the girls and hopefully help Mina find her way back home. This place felt so right.

Soon the house became quiet as Chloe and the children drifted off. Mina watched them as one by one they succumbed to the weariness of the day and fell into a deep sleep, then she rose and changed back into the elven garments that Theresa had given her.

Katie let out a little snore and several *popping* noises, as she was now dreaming, and Mina packed a small bag and crept toward the front door. She stopped and turned back toward Theresa. She watched her sleep for several moments, feeling great anxiety. Tears filled her eyes.

She placed her two fingers on her forehead and then Theresa's brow. Theresa moved slightly at the message being conveyed but continued sleeping.

Mina turned and exited the room. She silently opened the door. After looking back one last time, she closed it behind her. She listened to the sound of the rain, feeling the cold drops on her face as they mixed with the tears flowing down her cheeks. She could see her own breath.

The trees rustled all about her. She listened intently to them, clutching the key around her neck. Mina pulled the hood of her cloak over her head and set out toward the Black Forest alone.

Theresa awoke suddenly. Chloe was standing above her, looking very anxious. "Theresa, wake up!" she said again.

Theresa sprang up. "What... what's wrong?"

"The elf is gone! She left sometime during the night!"

"Not again," Theresa said, throwing off her blankets and hurrying out of the house, still in the nightgown that Chloe had loaned her. Her bare feet sank into the mud in the street from the heavy rain the night before, but Theresa took no notice of it or the chill in the air as she scanned the horizon all around her. Then she remembered... the message Mina had given her before leaving. *I'm going home. I will always love you as my own mum.*

"No, no, no!" Theresa cried aloud.

"Do you have any idea where she has gone... or why? Did we do something wrong?" Chloe's voice cracked.

"She's... she's still trying to get home! I guess she decided to go alone," Theresa said, her eyes still searching for anything moving near the Black Forest.

Mitchell approached with one other man. "I found her tracks leading toward the forest. By the way they have dissolved in the rain, I would guess she left around one this morning. She has a good head start on us. The wagon won't run in this mud, and we have only one other horse."

In the distance, Theresa spotted something moving away from the forest toward the village. It was too large to be Mina and brown in colour.

Mitchell looked at what Theresa was watching approach. It was moving fast. It was the other horse, the one Ned had taken to town with Theresa's letters for Melody and Medlock.

Something was wrong. The rider wasn't sitting upright. As Mitchell and several of the town's men hurried out to gather the galloping horse, Hilary emerged from the house, unfolding a blanket. She, Moiré, and Katie had been watching through the window.

Hilary draped the blanket over Theresa's shoulders as she had begun to shiver.

The men approached with the horse. Chloe's eyes grew wide as she clasped her hand to her mouth in horror. The rider had been tied to the horse, with severed harbinger vines around his feet and hands, binding them together. A separate vine was tied from his neck to the saddle horn, preventing him from sliding under the belly of the horse.

Mitchell instructed one of the men to take the animal and its rider to the stable. Rage filled his eyes.

"Ned's dead. All his ribs were crushed in on the left side. I'm guessing one of them punctured his lung or heart," he said grimly.

"Thomas," Theresa said, her voice quivering.

Mitchell nodded. "He must have circled back and ambushed Ned on his way from town."

Theresa began shaking. "Mina... Mina was heading toward the forest! If Thomas finds her, he'll do the same to her! Oh my God... We have to go after her!"

"Ready yourself. I'll saddle the other horse. We'll leave straightaway."

Chapter Twenty Two

Pursuit

HILARY AND KATIE watched in silence as Theresa prepared to depart with Mitchell. She hadn't even bothered to remove the crusted mud between her toes before donning her socks and boots.

Chloe and Moiré prepared food and water for Theresa and Mitchell to take with them as they didn't know how long they would be gone. As Theresa finished placing her possessions into her satchel, Hilary finally spoke. "Is Mina okay, Theresa?"

Theresa thought a moment before answering, giving a gentle, reassuring squeeze to Hilary's shoulder. "We'll find her. Don't worry. I need you both to be strong and do what Chloe tells you. Okay?"

"We want to go wif you!" Katie demanded.

"No. Not this time. But I'll be back… with Mina. There are only two horses, and we are going to have to travel fast to find her."

Katie continued protesting but to no avail.

Hilary grasped Katie by the shoulder as Theresa made her way to the doorway, whispering in her ear. Katie nodded, her protest stopping.

They watched through the window as Theresa and Mitchell mounted the horses. Mitchell's eyes flickered in flame, and his jaw was set tight. He was an expert at tracking animals—and people.

Theresa's eyes were filled with the same determination but also with fear for she knew what Thomas was capable of. Mud flew into the air from the horses' hooves as they sped off toward the Black Forest.

Chloe and Moiré soon left to join the other women as they needed to prepare Ned's body for burial.

Katie and Hilary quickly dressed and gathered a few supplies. As they donned their elven cloaks, Katie spoke in almost a whisper, fearing the empty house would hear her and ruin their plans.

"Hils, they are on horses. We're on foot. How will we find them?"

"We aren't following them to the Black Forest. Mina won't be there."

"Where will she be?" Katie asked with wide eyes.

"Remember her dream? She'll be at the cabin with him. We must get there first, before they do. We're her only chance."

The two girls quickly departed, heading southwest, back toward the cabin. The rain had begun again, slow but steady. The sky looked exactly like Mina had described in her dream.

Chapter Twenty-Three

Silence of the Trees

MINA TRIED TO survey her surroundings as she journeyed toward the ancient forest in hope that she would find the portal and be able to open it alone.

She checked the chain around her neck to make sure her key was still there. It was.

Her boots were caked with sticky mud several inches deep on the bottom. She felt like they weighed fifty pounds each; every step was difficult and clumsy. Mina used the stick she had been carrying for several miles to dig the mud out from the bottom of her boots again.

The hours passed in silence. She wondered if the trees were sleeping as she couldn't hear them except for the slow rain colliding with the new leaves that crowned them. Mina wasn't even sure if she was going in the right direction. All she had to go by was the occasional flash of lightning above her that would briefly light her path. Even the impossible wolves were silent tonight, sleeping in their dens, waiting out the storm. She was totally alone.

Bright veins of lightning displaced the darkness surrounding her. She was now in the foothills of the forest. Several large boulders flashed into view, startling the girl. There appeared to be an opening between them. Even though it was small, it would grant her some shelter from the rain.

Mina's hands pawed the rocks before her as if she were a blind mouse searching for a piece of cheese in a maze. Rain pelted her exposed face, and her clothes, soaked through, stuck to her skin. She fumbled along until another flash of lightning revealed the opening again, and she crawled into the small crevasse, relieved to find herself its only occupant. She was exhausted. She wished she had slept a bit before leaving but had feared she would oversleep and be caught before she could get a safe distance from the village. Peeking out of her sanctuary, she watched the rain pelt the ground, the branches and leaves of the trees becoming their own drumming orchestra.

She had to go home. There was no place for her in this world. She was neither loved nor wanted. She closed her eyes, shivering, and fell into a deep sleep.

Chapter Twenty Four

Realisations

T HERESA PATTED THE butt of her rifle again to confirm it was still with her. It was the very same rifle with which she had shot Chloe's toilet almost thirty years ago. She recognised the hand detailing in its stock when she thrust it into her saddle.

Tracking Mina toward the forest was slow going as most of her prints had dissolved in the rain. Impatience and panic swelled within her as time slipped away to prevent Mina's prophetic dream from becoming reality. The forest was thick with a cloying smell of trees, smothered by the musty aroma of earth and rot. It was as if time itself was restrained by its scent.

Theresa wondered why they had even bothered with the horses. They could have walked faster than this agonisingly slow ride as Mitchell studied the ground below and before him.

Every few minutes, he made an adjustment in their direction, causing fear to rise up in Theresa as she believed he had lost the trail. Impatiently she patted her rifle again.

"Thirty-two," Mitchell muttered quietly.

"What?" Theresa asked.

"That's how many times you have hit the butt of your rifle. It's not going anywhere. All you're doing is making yourself more anxious."

"You've lost the trail, haven't you?" she said in English, her voice cracking in fear.

Mitchell eyed at her with confusion. *"Cad é? Ní thuigim do focail?"*

Theresa shook her head, irritated with herself that she had forgotten to translate. *"Ar chaill tú an rian?"*

Mitchell shook his head. "The trail is strong. Look over at that tree stump. Do you see it?"

Theresa nodded.

"She stopped there to scrape her shoes."

Theresa studied the area surrounding the stump. Heavy prints led up to it, and lighter, more defined prints left the area with a pile of mud scraped onto the stump; she would never have caught that.

"Can we pick up the pace a bit? I don't think you realise just how critical time is right now."

Suddenly Mitchell changed direction, following another path unseen by Theresa. She followed him in confusion, patting her rifle again.

"I suspect she was using the lightning flashes to correct her path as she walked," he said.

"You're concerned about her dreams, aren't you?" Mitchell asked after a long moment of silence.

"Well, yes. Sometimes the details in her dream change, but it always ends the same. She dies in my arms… in the cold rain. It's raining, Wicky, and the rain is very cold." Theresa's last words were choked with emotion. "We have to hurry."

"Do you love her?" Mitchell asked.

"I… care about her," she said in an unconvincing tone.

Theresa felt transparent before this man, almost as if her soul were naked to him. She didn't like that feeling at all.

Mitchell pressed her again. "Do you… *love* her? Do you love her as your own?"

Theresa squirmed in her seat. "Yes. I love her… as if she were my own daughter. I love her."

He smiled. "Then there is yet hope. Have you told her?"

Theresa shook her head.

Mitchell nodded. "That is the most important thing you can do… that you must do. You must let her know you love her. Remember, she's the Hidden."

"I know, I know. The Unloved Sacrifice, I know." Her voice quivered.

"What do you think would happen if the Unloved Sacrifice became loved? Think upon it."

Theresa had no answer.

She silently wept as they travelled onward. She had finally admitted it, not only to Mitchell but to herself. She loved Mina as her own daughter. She truly loved her.

"I had a conversation with Chloe about Mina. You do realise Mina has sight. She's a seer," Mitchell said after a bit, displacing the awkward moment as Theresa's mind and heart marinaded in her own revelation.

"What? Yes, well, sort of. She has dreams that come true."

"What kind of dreams?"

Theresa shared the visions that had come to pass and how Mina had saved them numerous times.

"So, she used her dreams to alter the events that would have led to yours and the others' deaths, yeah?" Mitchell recapped.

"Well… sort of. They all happened just like she said, but she did—how can I put this?—manipulate the details to keep us safe."

"So perhaps we can manipulate the details to save her."

Theresa shook her head. "Every dream she's had has come true. In this dream, however, the details keep changing, but it always ends the same, her dying in my arms."

Theresa pulled up on her reins, her horse stopping suddenly. "Wicky, what if she's not a seer but a… creator or a manifestor?"

"What do you mean?"

"What if Mina is somehow bending reality in her dreams? What if her dreams aren't about reality, but her reality is about her dreams? We create our own realities. All of us do. What if she is subconsciously, with some unforeseen power she was gifted by this strange mer-elf blending, giving up on life because she's unloved? Could her dreams be creating this dark reality?"

Mitchell studied Theresa's face as her words echoed in his mind.

"The power of love is a most potent thing, especially a mother's love. But to have *never* been loved, that also has power, a horrible, negative power at that."

They rode on in silence for a time.

"Wicky, do you believe in reincarnation?" Theresa finally asked.

"Re— I don't know that word."

"That people come back over and over? Their souls returning to another body after death?"

"I believe in old souls if that's what you mean. Why?"

"Mina has had conversations with Lucy, my daughter who passed away, in her dreams. She knows things only Lucy knew, and she looks and acts a lot like her. I'm just wondering if maybe—"

Suddenly Mitchell stopped and dismounted his horse. He trudged through the mud to an outcropping of grey rocks. He seemed to follow an invisible path back and forth, missing something each time. After several passes, he stooped down onto his hands and knees, coating them in the dank squidge.

"What is it?" Theresa demanded. "What did you find?" She dismounted her horse and hurried toward the rocks.

Mitchell arose and headed back toward the horses, meeting her halfway. He pulled a short-blade knife from a leather sheath on his belt. A chill ran down Theresa's neck, but she sighed in relief when Mitchell began scraping the caked-on mud from each horseshoe of his beast with the knife.

"She took refuge in that small opening. I'm guessing she slept a fair amount of last night there as the newer tracks are firm. She might be close," he said with a stern look.

Theresa filled her lungs to call out to Mina. "Mi—!"

Mitchell quickly grasped her mouth to silence her, his eyes filled with fire. She could see Mitchell's blade out the corner of her eye.

Theresa's mind flashed back to Thomas, grasping her face in the same way before he slit her cheek open. She pulled away, feeling the same terror as she had all those years ago. She backed toward her horse and rifle, her eyes wide and body visibly shaking.

Mitchell, sensing her fear, took several steps back, slowly resheathing his knife.

"Theresa, there is a second set of prints," he said almost in a whisper as he pointed to the ground.

Theresa stopped her retreat and looked. Mitchell was right.

"They're fresh," he whispered.

"Thomas," she gasped, holding her hands to her mouth.

Mitchell nodded slowly. "These prints are deeper in the back, with little weight in the front. They are the prints of a man who is missing some toes."

They quietly stared into the dark forest for any sign of movement, fearing that Thomas's eyes were already upon them. Silently Mitchell and Theresa mounted their horses and crept farther into the darkness.

The trees were cloaked in a grey mist and a veil of rain. The forest floor was covered in a layer of moss, thick and deep. The horses' eyes moved about nervously as they stepped upon the dark carpet. It felt spongy to walk upon, almost as though something unnatural was waiting beneath to push its way up from the floor and consume them. The moss enveloped and climbed many of the surrounding trees and their branches as well. The trees not covered in moss were as black as night, their bark aged and weathered. These were creatures that had survived the fall of Rome, the Black Plague, and the burning of thousands of people who had been accused of witchcraft. They seemed to have eyes, eyes that were dark and brooding, passing judgement on everything and everyone that dared to cross their paths.

Voices seemed to come from the trees, ancient voices with whispered stories to tell. They were talking to them, warning them away.

The ground was a maze of roots as tall as a man and impossibly intertwined, creating an unnerving sense of claustrophobia. The darkness was absolute, far darker than night with only thin rays of light poking through the thick canopy above. A sense of awe mingled with great fear filled Theresa's heart as she looked upon the oldest forest in the world. This was indeed a Black Forest.

They would not be able to travel much farther on horseback. Soon they would have to track by foot. But whom would they be tracking, Mina or Thomas? Or were they themselves already being tracked?

Theresa rested her hand on her rifle as they vanished into the blackness.

Chapter Twenty Five

Katie and Hilary

"ADMIT IT! WE'RE lost!" Katie exclaimed.

"We are not lost. It's just taking longer to get back there," Hilary said defensively.

"We should have been there hours ago! We're going in circles, Hilary!" Katie was quite animated now, her face bright red.

"Theresa walked in a straight line to get to the village. We're walking in a straight line to get back," Hilary said very matter-of-factly.

"Snarflepoo!" Katie barked in anger. "See that rock? The big grey rock? I scratched me initials on it with a wee stone last time we passed it! Look!"

Hilary studied the boulder. *KC* had indeed been scratched on it.

"Don't you know the diffrenze between a straight line and a circle? Weren't you paying attention in school?" Katie flapped her arms, slapping them on her hips in dramatic display.

"Cor blimey," Hilary finally admitted. "We *are* going in circles. All right, Katie. Which way should we go?"

Her face still red, Katie pointed south. "I fink iz this way!"

Nearly another hour passed, but after topping the last hill, the cabin was finally in sight.

"Ole right, Hils. Now what do we do?"

Hilary had regained her composure. "We set traps. We don't have long to prepare."

Chapter Twenty Six

The Devil Above Her

S TRANGE SOUNDS FILLED the air as Theresa and Mitchell rode farther into the darkening forest. Unearthly echoes and whispers swirled about them, chilling them to the bone. Were the trees talking, Theresa wondered, or was it something much older, something darker?

The ancient trees creaked and moaned. Thick moss covered the branches as far up as they could see to the thick canopy of leaves that crowned the treetops. The air was chilled but still. Huge raindrops, dripping from the leaves of the trees above, made popping sounds as they impacted with the decaying leaves from years past and ferns covering the ground.

Theresa could see her breath.

Their very presence seemed to upset the silence that the trees demanded. No birds or insects were visible, but they could hear the scurrying sounds of small creatures moving about unseen along the lumpy ground. The thick ferns as tall as a man and with twisted roots were now impossible to navigate; they would have to walk from here.

A smell filled Theresa's nostrils, a smell she knew well. Theresa's and Mitchell's eyes met.

As they quietly reached for their rifles, a whooshing sound rang out around them. Theresa's horse reared onto its hind legs at the sound, but it was too late. A huge tree branch, tethered on both ends with rope, swung toward them. The log rammed into Mitchell's chest, ejecting him from his horse and depositing him nearly twenty feet away.

The log then impacted with the face of Theresa's horse, flipping the animal onto its side with her under it.

She lay motionless beneath the dying horse, unsure of what had happened, her head spinning. Theresa couldn't move. Her right leg was pinned under the beast.

The source of the foul smell approached her. She blinked several times, trying to bring her eyes into focus. As Theresa's mind cleared, she looked up; the Devil was standing above her.

"Hello, luvah!" Thomas smiled down at her with his brown teeth. "Miss me? Give us a kiss!" Sweat rolled down his nose and dripped into Theresa's mouth. She instantly spit it out in disgust.

"Wicky! Help me! Wicky!" she screamed.

Thomas laughed, rolling his head back in dramatic fashion. "Your new luvah can't help you, poppet. You into young men again? I'm afraid you killed another one off!"

"You murdered him, you bastard!" Theresa retorted, her voice filled with rage.

"I have to admit, he's much better-looking than that old sod you were with. I'd be tempted to shag this one."

Theresa felt sick inside. Just the sight of Thomas filled her stomach with nausea.

"You're mad, Thomas! You're a murderer too!"

Thomas stopped smiling and stooped down. He grasped her hair with his still-bloodied, bandaged hand and pressed his sweating forehead against hers.

"You killed Lucy! You killed *my* daughter!" he screamed, shaking her head by the hair.

Tears filled Theresa's eyes. "Don't you think I know that?" She covered her face with her hands and sobbed quietly.

Thomas stared down at her in silence. After a moment, he spoke in a quiet, almost whispered voice. "There, there. Don't worry, love. I'll put you out of your misery soon enough. One last thing. Where's that banshee of a child?"

"I-I don't know what you're talking about."

"That little shit that has caused me so much trouble. I've been following her trail for some time, and she's disappeared. Where is she?" Thomas demanded, his voice rising.

"She didn't disappear, Thomas. You're just a fucking poor tracker."

Thomas's bulging red eyes burrowed into Theresa, his upper lip twitching into a horrible contortion. Then he turned his attention to his surroundings. Mitchell's horse had bolted and was nowhere to be seen.

Theresa quietly grasped the butt of her rifle whilst Thomas was distracted. It wouldn't budge. At the angle she lay, she couldn't pull it free from beneath her horse.

Thomas looked down at her and smiled. "Let me help you with that, my love."

Within seconds, the rifle slid out and was now in his hands. He cocked the weapon and pointed it toward Theresa's face. Theresa closed her eyes.

Suddenly he pulled it back to inspect it. The end of the rifle was damaged, the barrel crushed in and bent slightly to the left. The gun was useless. Thomas looked at the rock beneath the horse that Theresa was lying next to. The impact against the rock and perhaps the stirrup had crushed the barrel.

"You haven't got a hacksaw on you, would you, love? No? No worries." He threw the rifle to the ground in anger and looked to where Mitchell lay crumpled in a pile, unmoving.

"Let's see what your luvah has on him, shall we?" As Thomas walked toward Mitchell, he turned back to Theresa. "Back in a mo. Don't go anywhere."

Thomas studied Mitchell's face. This was the man who threatened to shoot his balls off if he saw him again. Thomas sneered down at him. "I win," he said with glee in his voice.

After rummaging through Mitchell's clothes, Thomas stood, holding a knife—the very knife Mitchell had used to clean the mud from the horses' hooves just an hour ago.

Mina had watched in silent horror as the log crashed into Mitchell and Theresa's horse, crushing her beneath it. She felt so helpless. Mina had been hiding from the foul man for some time; it wasn't difficult for her as her elven instincts for making herself disappear took over. She could easily move through the forest in total silence; it was in her nature. The man was smelly and stupid. He was easily tricked onto a dead path, and she could smell him coming, both upwind and down. It had almost become a fun game for her.

When the man threw Theresa's rifle to the ground and began walking toward Mitchell, Mina moved toward Theresa. As Thomas rummaged through Mitchell's pockets, Mina silently peered over the belly of the twitching horse at Theresa below.

Theresa's eyes bulged from her sockets at the sight of the girl.

"Run, Lucy, run… and don't look back!" she whispered.

Mina pressed her knotted index finger against her lips. "Shhh." She studied the horse and the surrounding ground. "Where is your satchel?"

"Run, goddammit! He'll kill you!"

Mina slowly shook her head. "Where is the satchel?"

"It's under the leather flap on that side of the saddle!" Theresa whispered frantically.

Mina disappeared from Theresa's view for a moment only to return seconds later, holding the elven flute in her hands. Her eyes moved toward Thomas, who was now holding Mitchell's knife. He was smiling; he looked so happy.

Mina carefully placed the end of the wind instrument in her mouth.

"What are you doing, Mina?" Theresa hissed.

"Summoning the shadows. Be ready to move; it won't last long." She pressed the instrument to her lips again. Mina paused for a moment. "Make sure you keep your eyes open. Don't close them."

Theresa heard Thomas's voice in the distance. "On my way, luvah!"

A strange sound emanated from the instrument, a sound that Theresa had never heard before. It was a deep, grinding sound that made her body and even her teeth vibrate. She felt very strange. The sound seemed to alter everything around her. She closed her eyes, and a sudden wave of dizziness and nausea swept over her. She opened them again, and it dissipated.

The shadows seemed to come alive, swirling about them like dark tendrils of smoke, growing from the ground up and surrounding her and Mina. It was much like the darkness of night but made of shadow. The ground seemed to turn, as though a clock's hands were being adjusted and reset to correct the time. The raindrops suddenly were suspended in the air.

Theresa instinctively reached out and touched one. It exploded on her fingertip.

Mina placed her two fingers to her head and then onto the horse's brow. With great effort, the beast lifted itself up as though it were obeying a command.

Theresa pulled herself free by pushing back on the palms of her hands. Miraculously, she could see that she had fallen into a crevice between two rocks. Had she not landed in that exact place, her leg surely would have been crushed.

The horse collapsed back onto the ground, its breathing shallow and laboured. Even Theresa could tell that the animal was suffering terribly.

Mina again placed her fingers on the horse's brow. "I'm so sorry. Thank you," she whispered through tears to the animal. "You can rest now."

Theresa watched as the animal's face lost all expression and its eyes became blank. It breathed its last breath.

The ground moved again slightly, and the drops of rain slowly began their journey to the ground.

"We haven't much time. Can you walk?" Mina asked in a whisper.

Theresa nodded. Her knee hurt, but the pain was manageable. They hurried into the woods as the shadows lifted.

Thomas watched, frozen in time, as the ground surrounding his enemy was swallowed into shadow. The last thing he saw was what looked like Lucy, kneeling next to Theresa. After a moment, they disappeared like wisps of black smoke in the wind.

Chapter Twenty Seven

Mitchell

MITCHELL'S HORSE SLOWLY and warily wandered back toward his master. He looked about nervously for any more flying trees; he saw none. The horse nuzzled Mitchell with his nose and gave an occasional lick from his tongue. After a moment, the man stirred and opened his eyes.

Mitchell's vision was hazy. He lay in a daze, the trees above him the only thing he could focus upon. He could see his horse but only the outline of his blurry head. Mitchell struggled to breathe as he coughed up blood. Feeding his hand beneath his shirt, his fingers traced the gash in his side. Two sharp edges of bone protruded from his flesh. Like Ned, his ribs were broken; this must be the same trap that Thomas had used to kill Ned.

Mitchell grasped the stirrup on the horse's saddle and pulled himself up but soon collapsed back onto the ground. The pain was excruciating. Knowing what to expect, he tried again and managed himself onto the horse.

Mitchell sat hunched over the beast, trying to catch his breath before deciding his course of action. The reins were wrapped about his saddle's horn. After untangling them, he vomited more blood onto the ground, again gasping for air.

He studied his surroundings. He was alone. His heart sank when he spotted the downed horse that Theresa had been riding. Mitchell and his horse slowly strode over to where it lay. She was nowhere to be seen. Unable to focus on the ground to track her, he decided to head toward town. Melody hopefully was waiting for them there as they were well overdue to rendezvous.

Mitchell would gather the help necessary to form a rescue party. He vowed he would find her and end that man once and for all.

Chapter Twenty Eight

The Tree, the Choice

THERESA AND MINA found themselves on a narrow pathway that lay at the edge of a sharp precipice. A sheer drop of over twenty feet below them was covered in brambles, roots, deadwood, and scrub oak. The narrowness of the path made Theresa feel queasy as she peered down at it.

"I need to rest a moment, Mina. I need to sit!"

Mina helped her over to a large rock jutting out of the hillside. Theresa promptly plopped down, keeping her right leg straight before her. Her trousers were torn and frayed. She carefully pulled up her pant leg to inspect her knee. It was quite swollen and bruised.

"Will it be okay?" Mina asked with concern on her face.

Theresa nodded.

"Mina, what you did back there with the fluty thing and horse—that's very dark magic. Where did you learn that?"

Mina hung her head. "Útíradiel, the Augur, taught me how… to protect myself. The Aoileach people didn't like me. They called me a witch. They said I was evil because of the way I was made. Sometimes the other kids would hurt me or throw rocks at me. She taught me how to disappear."

"Mina, have you ever... hurt anyone?"

Mina's facial expression became one of guilt. "Only once."

"What did you do?"

A long silence preceded the child's confession. "Erm... Once at Saint Austin's, a boy was being mean to me."

A memory that Mina had shared with her flashed through Theresa's mind. She remembered seeing the boy on the school grounds and the emotion she felt at the sight of him. He was the boy that had coaxed Mina into the cellar and locked her in after promising her chocolate.

"Arthur?"

"Yes. How did you know?"

"That was one of the memories you shared with me."

"Oh," Mina said.

"What did you do to Arthur?"

"He poured some black ink into my tea during breakfast. I didn't know it, so it turned my lips and teeth black for a week and made my tummy very sick. The other kids made sport of me."

"What did you do to Arthur, Mina?"

Mina was silent for a long moment before blurting out her revenge.

"I hit him on the head with a bit of wood!"

Theresa laughed in relief. "Sounds like he deserved it!"

"After that, they locked me downstairs with the rats."

Theresa took the girl in her arms and wrapped her in a warm embrace.

Theresa looked at her surroundings. "Mina, I think we are lost."

Mina shook her head. "We're not. We've been doing lots of loops to lose that man. I think he's lost now. I haven't smelled him for some time."

Theresa let out a small laugh. "He needs a bath for certain!"

"He's a fucking poor tracker too." Mina repeated Theresa's words from the earlier confrontation with Thomas.

"Don't say that word, Mina. It's a bad word!"

"But you said it. What does it mean?"

"I was very cross with Thomas. I shouldn't have said that. I didn't know you overheard us. I'm sorry. Please don't use that word again, okay?"

Mina nodded, not fully understanding.

"Theresa, why did you call me Lucy?"

"I'm sorry. It wasn't intentional. You resemble my daughter in many ways, even your personality. It just slipped out," Theresa answered, finally acknowledging it to herself.

"Oh. Is it bad that I resemble her?"

Theresa smiled and shook her head. "No, it's not bad." She stared at the girl's face for a moment. "Mina, this will sound strange, but I need to ask you. But I don't know the proper words. Is Lucy... or perhaps part of Lucy—her soul—in you?"

Mina cocked her head. "Um, no. I'm just Mina." A look of hurt came over the child's face. "Could you love me if Lucy *was* inside me... and not just... me?"

"Oh, honey!" Theresa quickly wrapped her arms around Mina and held her tight. "I'm sorry! I'm so sorry. It had nothing to do with that." Theresa bared her heart. "Mina, when Lucy died, part of me died inside. It left a terrible pain that never goes away. Like you once said to me, I have an empty place inside now. I think you have that same empty place too. Am I right?"

Mina's eyes filled with tears as she nodded.

Theresa held her in her arms as they both cried. "Mina, I need to tell you something, how I feel about..."

Suddenly Mina broke her grasp and stood, a look of disbelief on her face. "We're here! The tree is just up this hill! It's the way home! I wondered why the other trees told me to go this way!" She helped Theresa up, and they ascended the hill.

Theresa stood in awe at the scene before her. It was unlike anything she'd ever seen or imagined. Blackened rocks surrounded them, looking like the aftermath of a great war or perhaps the surface of a dead planet. Apart from one scorched tree, the area was lifeless.

The tree before her must have once been glorious. It was ancient, with a door—not carved but somehow grown separately in its base. The door was small and made of oak, and one would have to stoop low to get through the entrance.

A keyhole was set within a small metal ring, with an inscription engraved upon it. The artwork boasted of Celtic influence, though it was old and tarnished. The tree itself looked dead and had fallen into decay, blackened from fire and disease. Much of the bark was shredded into what resembled course hair and danced in the breeze. A single root, which had split the rock in two, held the rest of the tree in place, preventing it from toppling over the ravine so precariously near its edge. That single remaining root was its last lifeline.

"This tree doesn't look so good. It might not work anymore."

Mina nodded whilst grasping the key around her neck.

Theresa wrapped her arm around the stunned girl, trying to comfort her. "Mina, what is left for you there? You have no family, no one there who cares for you. You were just a tool to them. Why would you want to go back there? What I'm trying to tell you is I lo—"

"I can't go anyway," Mina said in resignation.

"You have the key, Mina, and I'm here to open it for you. If you want me to, I'll take you home.

"I know, but I *can't* go right now," Mina confessed.

"Why? If it's really what you want—"

"Hilary and Katie are in danger… from Thomas."

"Love, the girls are safe, back in the village."

Mina shook her head. "They went back to the cabin alone this morning."

"Why? How do you know that?"

"I dreamt it. We have to go there to help them. That's where we've been heading since we lost that man."

Theresa searched her mind for answers. "Why would they go there?"

Mina shook her head. "Maybe they were trying to prevent my other dream from coming true. I dunno."

"Did the rest of it still happen?"

Mina nodded.

"Shit," Theresa said to herself, realising that their attempt to help Mina might have been another in a long list of events that were moving them toward this inevitable fate.

"Isn't *shit* a bad word too?"

"Yes, yes. It's a bad word too. Sorry."

"Theresa?" Mina said after a moment.

"Yes, love."

"We have to get there soon."

Theresa surveyed the scenery below, then pointed. "That way. Yeah?"

Mina nodded.

Chapter Twenty Nine

Bait and Lure

"YOU SHOH 'BOUT this, Hils?" Katie asked sceptically.

"If you have a better idea, now is the time," Hilary answered. "Do you understand my plan, Katie?"

"I understand it betta than you do."

Hilary raised her eyes, glaring at Katie. "You have to run fast, very fast. If he sees you duck into the wrong doorway, it'll fail miserably. He must believe you went into the doorway that leads to the port. I'll shut him inside and latch the bolt, but you must be quick!"

"I know! He couldn't catch me before when he had toes. How's he going to catch me now, wifout?" Katie said defensively.

"Umm… Katie, he did catch you. Remember?"

"Shut up. Wif ole the exercise we've been getting lately, I reckon I can run even fasta now!"

"I hope so… for all our sakes," Hilary said.

"Hils, what makes you fink he'll take the bait?"

"Hope," Hilary admitted.

"Tha's it? Hope?"

"That's it. Let's get upstairs so we're not caught by surprise. You rigged the plank to collapse on the boat, yeah?"

Katie nodded. "Two steps an' down he goes into the black water! You shoh that big door will 'old 'im?"

Hilary nodded in return. "He'll never get that door open from the inside; I removed the lever. We lure him in, lock it proper, and he'll be in there forever. No one dies today, Katie."

"Shhh," Katie said. "Did you hear that?"

"What?"

"I heard sumpfin."

Up in Smoke

THERESA AND MINA sipped rainwater that had pooled on a nearby rock. It had been several hours since they had emerged from the forest. The cabin should have only been a short walk from the foothills, but they had emerged on the far-east end of the Black Forest and were forced to walk along the moors as Theresa's knee was swollen and could bear little weight. She had fashioned a walking stick to aid her, but the journey back to the cabin was taking much longer than they had hoped.

They walked in silence, not only from exhaustion but from the fear each of them silently held of being too late to help Katie and Hilary.

The slow, steady rain had soaked them to the bone. Rain had filled the hood of Mina's cloak. It sloshed about as she walked, often pouring down the back of her neck and back. Her teeth chattered, and her face had a pale, bluish hue to it.

Theresa sniffed the air. She sniffed several more times, each time seeming more anxious.

"I smell wood burning," she said.

Mina nodded, her face looking grim. They hurried over the top of the last hill and looked down upon that which was filling their nostrils and now stinging their eyes. The cabin was burning in the valley below. Thick smoke blanketed the area like a low-lying ground fog.

"No," Mina gasped.

Theresa took a long look around the landscape before they began their descent down the hill. She saw no sign of Thomas or of Hilary or Katie.

Mina, not watching the path before her, slipped and fell face-first into the sticky mud. Theresa helped her to her feet, but Mina's face and hands were now coated in the goo. She used the end of Mina's cloak to clear the girl's eyes.

As they approached, the view of the cabin was intermittently obscured by the thick smoke. The rain had controlled much of the fire, but the cabin was now just a blackened shell with no signs of life in it.

"Oh God. Oh God," Theresa kept saying over and over, her hand cupped in front of her mouth. She hurried into the smouldering debris, rummaging through the remains of the cabin, frantically looking for any signs of Katie or Hilary. She found herself turning in circles amidst the smouldering embers, more relieved each minute she didn't find their remains.

Her eyes moved to the back room. The passage to the tunnel was open. She limped down the long brick corridor, shaking in fear as she peered into each room for the girls. The thick smoke burned her eyes and lungs. No sign of Katie or Hilary.

There was one last place to look: the big wooden door leading to the staircase and dock below. She climbed over the collapsed ceiling timbres as she made her way toward the big door.

Suddenly fire erupted behind her.

Chapter Thirty One

The Dream Realised

M INA'S HEART BEAT in her chest, pulsing through her body and down to the ends of her fingertips. She was so alone. She was so afraid.

She closed her eyes and listened to the sound of the trees pleading with her to return to them. Mina's heart was racing.

She slowly turned about and shivered.

The man was now standing before her. "You look like her... but you're not her. Are you, poppet?"

Mina shook her head.

"What the fuck are you?" he screamed through sneering lips.

"Fuck is a bad word, don't you know," Mina said quietly.

"Well, aren't you an arrogant little shit?"

"Shit's a bad word too."

Thomas took several steps toward her and stared into her eyes, cocking his head in an animallike fashion. He grasped her face. "Where is she?"

"Get your hands off my daughter, you sick bastard!"

Thomas turned toward the voice. Theresa stood before him, covered in soot, her clothes burned, her hair singed from the fire. A fierce rage filled Theresa's eyes.

Hilary and Katie stood stone-faced on either side of her. They were shaken but whole.

For a moment, fear shone in Tom's eyes. He had never seen or heard this kind of resolve in Theresa before. He pointed Mitchell's knife at Mina. "Your daughter? This little bag of bones?" He laughed cruelly. "Who'd you have this one with, a retarded circus midget?"

"Get. Away. From my daughter. This is between you and me," Theresa said, her voice bursting with barely controlled anger.

"You killed my daughter, I kill yours. Fair is fair, eh, luvah?" Thomas smiled with his brown teeth as Mina trembled in fear.

Suddenly a woman's voice called out from the darkness. "Mina!"

As Mina turned toward the sound, a loud *bang!* punctured the silence of the rain. Thomas dropped to the ground, facedown in the muddy water, the knife still in his hand.

Katie and Hilary stood motionless in shock at Thomas lying crumpled in the mud, a bullet through his temple.

A figure emerged from the haze. It was Mitchell, rifle in hand, looking weak but very much alive. Behind him was Melody, holding the reins of two horses.

"Mel? Wicky... You're alive!" Theresa said, unable to believe her eyes.

Melody smiled at her. "Howdy." She looked down at Thomas. "God, I hate this prick."

Theresa embraced Melody and Mitchell, tears flowing from her eyes.

"It's over. It's over," Melody said with a comforting smile.

"Mel, how did you find us?" Theresa asked after regaining control of her emotions.

"Your friend, Mitchell!" she said with a smile. "He was in pretty bad shape when we met at the rendezvous point, but fortunately for him, I'm a nurse. I set his ribs, taped them up, and he was ready to come back out here. He's a keeper! Looks like we got to the party just in time."

Theresa staggered for a moment, looking faint. The adrenaline in her body was subsiding.

"What's wrong with your leg?" Melody demanded.

"A horse fell on it. I'm okay. I just need to sit down."

"*Beidh orainn campa a chur ar bun anseo night. Tá sé ródhéanach dul ar ais go dtí an sráidbhaile,*" Mitchell said in a weak, raspy voice.

Theresa nodded. "*Tá na seomraí fós slán. Sílim gur smaoineamh an-mhaith é sin.*"

"What was that?" Melody asked.

"Mitchell says we should stay here tonight. I couldn't agree more!" Theresa paused and looked into Melody's eyes. "How were the two of you able to communicate?"

Melody let out a laugh. "We weren't! But a shopkeeper at the dry goods place speaks both languages. He translated what Mitchell was saying and the danger you were in. He even loaned us a horse, and we left immediately. I told him he should stay and rest, but he refused. He's a very stubborn man!"

"How did you find us?"

"He knew right where to go, and we followed the smoke," Melody replied.

"Ahem!" Hilary cleared her throat, having grown tired of the conversation and being ignored.

"Oh yes, of course. Melody, I want you to meet my dear friends, Hilary and Katie!"

Melody hugged both their necks. "It's a delight to meet you!"

"You're American?" Hilary asked.

"Why yes! I am! A California girl!" she said, smiling kindly.

Theresa continued, "And of course Mina."

They looked toward the last place Mina had stood. Theresa gasped.

Mina was lying on her back in the mud, motionless, her leg folded beneath her.

"Mina!" Theresa screamed in horror as they hurried over to where she lay.

She gathered the child into her arms, holding her close. Mina looked ghostly pale, but her eyes remained open.

"No! No! This can't be happening!" Theresa muttered as she caressed the girl's cheeks, clearing Mina's hair from her face with a trembling hand.

"Mina, I need to tell you. I haven't told you before. Mina, I love you. I love you as my own daughter! You need to know that, Mina! I love you as my own daughter!"

"I... would have been a good..." The girl's eyes slowly closed, dispelling the tears that had filled them. The tears trickled down her cheeks and vanished onto the ground as her heart beat its last. Darkness engulfed her in silence as breath left her body.

The only sound now was that of the rain. Theresa cradled Mina in her arms, rocking her gently as her own tears caressed the child's cheeks. She sang a lullaby to her as the darkness descended.

Chapter Thirty Two

The Longest Night

T HUNDER RUMBLED OVERHEAD as Melody knelt to check Mina's pulse. She sorrowfully closed her eyes as her head dropped. Melody lifted the child's body from Theresa's desperate grasp as the mourning mother wept and examined the knife wound on Mina's back. Blood was still pouring from it.

Melody quickly removed her scarf and held it against the wound. "Hold this here. Push hard!" she demanded.

Theresa remained unmoved.

"Theresa! Snap out of it, goddammit! Hold this against the wound as I lay her down! Theresa!"

Theresa finally responded, sensing Melody's frantic haste.

Melody made a fist with both hands and struck the child's chest. She breathed into her mouth several times and rechecked her pulse. After a moment, she nodded to herself. She hurriedly wrapped the scarf around Mina's back and abdomen, knotting it tightly.

"We have to get her someplace dry and warm!" Melody shouted, looking about desperately.

"What about the boat?" Katie suggested in a quivering voice.

"Boat?" Melody looked all about, uncertain she had heard Katie correctly.

Theresa barked out orders to Mitchell in the old language. Despite his broken ribs, he managed to lift the girl from the ground. They hurried into the remains of the cabin, Hilary leading the way.

The long brick corridor was difficult to negotiate, but the fire, with help from the rain, had nearly burned itself out.

Theresa limped ahead of Mitchell, climbing over the smouldering support beams. Melody continued massaging the child's heart.

Mitchell winced in pain as he stretched out over the pile of wood timbers to hand Mina to Theresa.

They hurried down the stairs, Hilary and Mitchell in the lead, Theresa in agony from the additional weight on her knee and the descent of the steep stairs.

Hilary quickly relit the torches, revealing the details of the vast underground portal.

Melody's eyes grew wide at what lay before her. Never in her wildest dreams had she conceived of such a place.

Theresa calmly reassured the child in her arms. "Hold on, baby. I love you. Hold on."

Suddenly a section of the old, decaying wood tread broke loose as Theresa stepped down. She lost her balance, landing on her side, but maintained her hold on Mina's arm as the girl's seemingly lifeless body hung over the edge of the stairs, still nearly fifteen feet from the cavern floor.

"Wicky! Help! Wicky!" she cried out, feeling her grasp on Mina slipping.

Mitchell hurried down the remaining stairs and positioned himself below Mina. *"Lig dul! Tá sí agam!"*

"Don't you drop her, Wicky! *Nach scaoileann tú í!"* Theresa sobbed.

"Lig dul!"

Theresa's eyes flooded with tears as she released Mina, but Mitchell was sure-handed and gathered the girl into his arms. He instantly crumpled to the ground in agony but kept Mina safe in his grasp until the others joined him on the cavern floor.

Theresa regathered the child into her arms as Hilary tended to Mitchell.

As Theresa and Melody approached the plank to the *Círtolthiel,* Katie cried out, "Theresa! Stop! It's a trap!"

Theresa stopped one step short of the rigged plank and turned back to Katie with fury in her eyes.

"That plank was supposed to be a trap for Thomas, but he never came down here! It will collapse if you step on it!" Katie explained as Hilary and Mitchell hastened another plank onto the boat.

They boarded the ship, negotiated the maze of splintered wood and tangled rigging across the deck, and hurried down the stairs to the captain's cabin below. Hilary quickly swept the items on the captain's table onto the floor with a clatter.

Melody was so lost in awe at the sights that surrounded her she didn't hear Theresa calling her.

"Oi! Mel!" Katie finally barked out after Theresa's failed attempts to get her attention. "Mina needs you… *now!*"

Melody snapped out of her trance and attended Mina's bedside. She checked the girl's pulse. It was so faint she could scarcely feel it. She let out a sigh as a grim look covered her face.

"She's lost so much blood." Melody looked about frantically for anything she could use to help stem the bleeding. "Needle and thread. I need a needle and thread!"

Everyone instantly complied and began searching the cabin for a medical kit, except for Mitchell.

"Theresa! *Cad atá á lorg againn?*" he said frantically.

"*Ní mór dúinn ar threalamh fuála! Tá sí chun* stop a *chur leis* and bleeding!" Theresa replied without looking back.

Mitchell joined in the search, opening a cupboard and frantically fumbling through it.

"*Fuair sé!*" he cried out, holding up the sewing kit.

Melody quickly snatched it from Mitchell and began threading a needle with the elven thread, trying to stop her blood-covered hands from shaking. "We're going to need lots of clean water and towels!"

Katie and Hilary looked at each other. "We're on it!" They both rushed out, hoping the supplies needed would still be in the loo upstairs and hadn't burned with the cabin.

"Theresa, I'm going to gather the horses and have a look about for any other supplies we can use. I brought some food and water. I'll be back in a bit," Mitchell said weakly, holding his side.

Theresa nodded with an appreciative smile. "Thank you, Wicky."

"I didn't know you spoke another language, Theresa," Melody said.

"Nor did I."

"Where did you learn it?"

"It is actually my native tongue. I just… forgot."

"How can you forget something like that?"

Theresa paced back and forth, wiping back the endless tears with her blood-covered hands.

She had never had the opportunity to watch Melody work before, though she wished it was under different circumstances. Theresa was usually tending their home whilst Melody worked at the hospital, treating the soldiers' battle wounds. She felt such admiration for her friend at this moment. There was no one more qualified for this right now than Melody.

Theresa felt nauseated as she watched Melody sewing the wound closed. She had tried so hard to prevent this. She had tried to anticipate every possibility and every variable and prepare for them. But in the end, she had still been powerless to stop Mina's dream from coming to pass.

"Incredible," Melody muttered.

"What?" Theresa snapped to attention.

"This medical kit, the suture and needle. It's incredible. We could really use stuff like this in the hospital. The wound is literally sealing with each stitch."

"It's made by elves, woods elves. I doubt if it's available for purchase in London," Theresa said flatly.

Melody stopped for a split second and looked at Theresa. "Elves?" she said with disbelief in her voice. "What is this place? It's like an underground seaport?"

"This is an elven ship. It's called the *Círtolthiel,* and it is a portal, or was, to the world Mina and I are from."

"Huh?"

"I'm from her world, Melody. She was telling the truth. I was sent here as a child to prepare for Mina's return. I'm not even British. In fact, my name isn't even Theresa," she said, her voice cracking.

"What's your name then? Are you a mermaid or elf?"

Theresa winced at the condescension in Melody's voice. "Well, it's actually Treena if you really must know, and I'm not mer or woods elf. My mother was an Arapaho Indian, and my dad was Aoileach."

"Aoileach?"

"It's a derogatory term for the native peoples."

Melody stared at her for a moment. "Tree, you need to get some rest. Seriously."

"It's a long story. I'll tell you about it later," Theresa said with a sigh.

"Can't wait to hear this one."

Soon the girls returned with towels and several basins of clean water as well as blankets and a pillow for Mina. The items smelled of smoke but were in otherwise good condition.

"The lavatory is still usable. We can still draw water," Hilary announced. "We might even be able to sleep in our rooms if we can get the smoke smell out."

"That's great news, Hils. Thank you. Thank you both," Theresa replied.

"Speaking of smell, what is that god-awful stench?" Melody asked as she tied and snipped off the last stitch.

"When the portal closed, the water inside became stagnant and was poisoned from the basalt towers in this cavern. I suspect there are also some strange minerals in here as well. That's why it smells so bad," Katie said.

Melody and Theresa carefully cleaned Mina's wounds and bloodstained skin. Melody checked the girl's pulse and breathing. She closed her eyes and released a long sigh.

"Is she going to be okay?" Theresa asked, looking drained and exhausted.

"Tree… I don't know. She's very weak, and she's lost so much blood. She has a pulse, but her heart…" Melody shook her head. "You have to be prepared that she might not make it through the night."

Theresa's eyes filled with tears as she seemed to shrink before Melody's eyes. Melody held her close as Theresa wept.

Mitchell returned, looking pale and grim.

"Wick, what's the news?" Theresa said, quivering as she fought back the tears. "Sorry. *Cad é an nuacht*, Wicky?"

"The bedrooms are usable, but we'll have to take turns on watch. I'll take first watch." He looked exhausted and in great pain.

"What's happened? Why do we need someone on watch?"

Mitchell sighed; it was obvious he didn't want to share the news. "I went to gather the horses for the night. One's gone. I went back to where I put Thomas down. He's gone as well. I don't understand how it can be. His wound was mortal, but just in case, we should stand watch. More than likely he just rode off and died, but this feels very dark somehow. It's not natural. The good news is he didn't take the horse that I packed food on. The bad news is he now has my rifle. How is the elf child?"

Theresa shook her head. "She's alive. We'll have to wait and see."

"What did he say?" Melody asked after Mitchell left.

"Thomas is gone. He took one of the horses."

"Shit," Melody mumbled. "Theresa, you need some sleep. I'll stay with her."

"We can't move her to her room?"

Melody shook her head. "She can't be moved right now. Get some rest."

"No. I'm staying with her."

"Tree, you can't do anything for her now."

"Yes, I can," Theresa said, sobbing. "I can be here. I can hold her in my arms one last time and tell her I love her, whatever happens. This time I *can* be here!"

"Okay. Let me have a look at that knee first."

The night was agonisingly long for Melody and Theresa. Melody had to frantically restart the child's heart again, as it stopped several hours postsurgery. The two women then took turns monitoring her pulse with their fingers pressed to her neck or wrist whilst the other attempted to sleep.

Theresa continuously whispered her love and future plans for them into Mina's ear. She knew the girl was unconscious but still hoped her words would somehow be heard and give Mina a reason and the strength to live.

The Morning After

T HE MORNING BROUGHT sunshine though a brisk chill remained in the air. Ground fog covered the area in a strange eerie and silent mist.

Mitchell had remained at his post throughout the night despite severe pain and not a wink of sleep in over twenty-four hours.

Katie and Hilary both awoke early and silently descended the stairs to find out if Mina had survived the night. After almost stepping on the false plank again, Katie pulled the rigged plank free and discarded it into the depths below, cursing it with several discourteous Katie-isms.

As Hilary was the quieter of the two, she crept into the captain's quarters, taking a deep breath of anticipation before entering the room. Melody slept soundly on the captain's cot. Theresa sat slumped over in a chair next to Mina, asleep with her head resting on her arms.

Hilary looked to Mina. Her head was turned away, so she crept round the table, holding her breath for fear of what she might find.

Colour had returned to her face, and she seemed to be sleeping.

Hilary let out a sigh of relief. Mina opened her eyes and smiled. "Good morning," she whispered.

Hilary's eyes filled with tears. "Good morning, Mina!"

"Hilary, what are you doing?" Theresa demanded in a groggy, half-asleep voice as she lifted her head from the table.

"She's awake!" Hilary exclaimed. "Mina's awake!"

Melody rose and attended Mina's bedside, checking her pulse and her forehead for any sign of fever. She smiled. "Welcome back, Mina!"

Theresa wrapped her arm around Mina's shoulder and placed her face next to the child's. "Hi!" she whispered, tears welling up in her eyes.

"Hi, Theresa," Mina said with a weak smile.

"Mum. Call me Mum," Theresa replied.

Mina's eyes filled with tears, and her bottom lip began trembling.

"Hey! I have something for you." Theresa reached into her trousers pocket. She pulled out the small heart necklace and placed it around Mina's neck.

"Lucy… your… sister, said I could share it with you. It's from her."

Mina smiled, tears welling in her eyes. "Sister? Thank you. If I dream of her again, I'll make sure to tell her thanks too."

"Tree," Melody said in a near whisper, recognising the necklace. "My bag."

Theresa crunched her eyebrows together as Mel showed her the contents of her bag, then smiled and nodded.

"This is for you as well," Theresa said, presenting the rag doll to Mina.

Mina wrapped her arm around the doll and pulled her close.

"Your name is Judy," she whispered, drifting off to sleep.

"You went back there, didn't you?" Melody said angrily. "I told you not to, but you did it anyway. That's what started this whole mess, isn't it?"

"Not now, Mel. What's done is done. Let it go, okay?"

Hilary quietly exited the room and shared the good news with Katie. Both girls held each other, crying tears of joy before heading back upstairs.

Katie relieved Mitchell from his post and managed to convey to him that Mina was better. She then helped him into a bedroom and onto the bed for some well-deserved sleep and took his place on watch.

Meanwhile, Hilary took it upon herself to prepare a meal from the supplies that Mitchell had brought and a few surviving items from the cabin. The coal-burning stove had survived, along with just enough coal to fire up the stove for one last meal. She managed to find enough ingredients to make pancakes, adding some of the dried berries that Mitchell had packed in his saddle and melted down some hard packed brown sugar from one of the pantry shelves for syrup.

She first prepared breakfast for Mina, then Theresa, Melody, Katie, then herself, choosing to let Mitchell sleep a bit. She made multiple trips up and down the long stairway to the *Círtolthiel*, bringing each of them food and drink one at a time.

By early afternoon, Melody decided it was safe to move Mina upstairs to a proper bed.

Theresa stayed with the sleeping child throughout the day, singing songs to her and telling her stories about the American Civil War and her people, the Arapaho, fighting for survival during the battle of Sand Creek.

Mina spoke very little and drifted in and out of sleep for most of the day, but just the sound of her mother's voice comforted her and kept her spirits high.

Hilary attended to Mitchell's needs, bringing him food and drink. After she offered to fluff his pillow for the tenth time, he excused her to get some much-needed rest of her own.

Near dusk, Mitchell resumed his post to stand guard for the night. In the morning, they would return to the village to finish recuperating there.

He looked forward to seeing his son Yavin. Just a day earlier, he had feared he would never see him again. A sense of relief and peace filled him, and he felt very fortunate that this nightmare was at an end.

As the night descended, Melody and Theresa settled into bed with Mina between them for some desperately needed sleep. Theresa's knee throbbed, but the pain was subsiding to the point of being tolerable. She hoped the magical elven blankets would help her sleep through the night. Within moments of pulling the covers up to her chin, she felt herself growing sleepy.

Melody broke the wonderful spell by striking up a conversation with her, the first proper conversation they had had since being reunited.

"Have you looked in the mirror today?" she whispered so as not to wake Mina.

"I'm sure I look dreadful," Theresa replied, her eyes growing heavy.

"No, I'm serious. Have you seen your face?"

"No. Why?" she replied.

Melody gently ran her fingertips along Theresa's scar. Theresa recoiled as she hated being touched there.

"Your scar has faded... considerably."

"What?"

"Look at my hands," Melody instructed. "Do they look any different?"

Theresa studied the back of Melody's hands with growing curiosity. "Actually, they do. The liver spots are all gone."

"My arthritis is gone too. Look at my fingers," Melody added.

"They look ten years younger."

"So does your scar. It's not red anymore. In fact, I can barely see it. The top and bottom don't fold in at the line when you talk either."

"What's going on?" Theresa ran her fingers along the scar. It certainly felt different.

"I dunno. But I do know both my hands and your face were covered in blood... Mina's blood." Melody shrugged.

"You think there is something in her blood?"

Melody shrugged again. "Just... Who is she? *What* is she?"

Theresa gave Melody the condensed version of who and what the Hidden Child was. To her surprise, Melody seemed open to what she was hearing, very unlike how she had responded to the child's claims back home all those weeks ago.

They lay in silence afterward, trying to process the connection between Mina and the strange healing they had both experienced in their bodies. Soon the power of the elven blanket became too much to resist, and their thoughts stilled. Deep sleep overtook them.

Chapter Thirty Four

Blame

MITCHELL AWOKE TO the sound of wood being chopped with an axe. He momentarily felt anger with himself for having dozed off at his post, but he reasoned that under the circumstances, he had done well to have lasted as long into the night as he did.

He felt rested but quite sore and found it nearly impossible to take deep breaths without his ribs being displaced and causing great pain. He slowly and stiffly rose to investigate what Theresa was working on, axe in hand.

"Good morning," he said in a gravelly voice.

"Hi," she said with a smile.

"How's the knee?"

Theresa smiled. "Better! Thanks for asking. Your ribs?"

"What are you working on?" He ignored her question as he looked down at the odd rectangular frame she'd constructed.

"It's going to be a carrier of sorts to put Mina on. She's not in any condition to walk or even ride on the horse."

"Oh, good idea. Like a stretcher?" he asked.

"Actually, it will be drawn by the horse. American Indians used something like this many years ago. I'll stretch a blanket over the frame, and we can secure Mina to it."

Mitchell nodded. "Good idea."

With that, he turned and headed back toward the cabin ruins. He passed Katie and Hilary, who were headed toward Theresa, carrying several blankets.

"Will these work?" Hilary asked, her countenance downcast.

Theresa nodded with a smile. "Thank you."

The two girls stood silent as Theresa began slicing one of the blankets into long strips to be fastened onto the frame.

"What's on your mind, girls?"

Katie finally spoke. "This is ole our fault, innit?"

"Why do you say that?"

There was deep shame in her voice, and her eyes teared up.

Hilary realised Katie couldn't continue and took the lead. "Erm... If we hadn't disobeyed you and come here, this wouldn't have happened, would it? Mina nearly dying is because of us, isn't it?"

Theresa stood motionless, staring at nothing. After gathering the proper words, she turned to the girls. She hobbled several steps toward them and took them into her arms. They both began sobbing.

"Katie, Hilary, look at me."

Their eyes were filled with remorse and guilt.

"I've never been one to believe in such things as destiny or fate, but as hard as we tried these past few weeks, months—however long it has been now—to change things, in the end, we did. This is the way it had to happen to save Mina and stop Thomas. We all had roles to play in this scripted drama, and we each fulfilled our part to the best of our ability. Mina is alive, and we are alive. Let's be grateful for that, yeah?"

Katie began sobbing again. "Mr Tuhly isn' alive. He's dead."

Theresa gently lifted Katie's chin up and looked lovingly into her eyes. "Tad had a role to play too, and he gave it everything he had. He gave his life so that we could live. We can honour him for his sacrifice and hold our memories of him in our hearts forever."

The three held each other, finally releasing the pain of their loss.

Chapter Thirty Five

Black Warning

I T WAS EARLY afternoon before the wounded troop set off for the village.

Mina had been carefully secured to the frame behind the horse and made as comfortable as possible. She held Judy tightly against her neck. She quipped that she now knew how Turly's pipe felt, sitting in his shirt pocket.

Melody and Theresa talked briefly before they embarked about how quickly the child seemed to be recovering from her injury. Melody even noted that Mina's heart sounded stronger and more regular than it had before; but further tests would be needed to confirm that. Even the swelling from the arthritic knots of her fingers and toes seemed to be subsiding, something Melody noted as being impossible.

Theresa had her own theory. She remembered her conversations with Chloe and Mitchell about the power of a mother's love, especially regarding the Hidden Child: a poorly created and impossible blend of mer and elf-kind who was not meant to live very long.

Could a mother's love—Theresa's love for this child who had never been loved—be undoing the damage to her body? Was a mother's love, her love, *that* powerful?

Mitchell and Theresa had a bit of a row over who would ride the horse back to the village, each demanding that the other take the saddle because of their respective injuries. Mitchell prevailed, but with the provision that Hilary lead the horse with Theresa riding so as not to put further strain on his own ribs from holding the reins.

Theresa gingerly mounted the horse and decided to ride sidesaddle as the inward stress on her knee from the overfed horse was quite unpleasant.

They journeyed in silence, lost in their own thoughts. As the adrenaline subsided from their bodies, they felt weary and drained, especially Theresa. She knew her life could never be the same. She was a different person now. She had been forced to face her demons of loss and abuse. She felt free—not only from her past but free to love again. Mina had awakened something in her she had thought long dead... the ability to love. Theresa daydreamed about their future together, mother and daughter. She even found herself daydreaming about Wick Mitchell. Was it possible that she had feelings for him and he still for her?

As they reached the top of the last hill, Mitchell paused. Thick black harbingers covered the ground nearly a foot deep between them and the village. He sniffed the air suspiciously, sensing something foul.

He walked back toward Theresa and Melody. Theresa knew that stern look that had suddenly filled his eyes.

"*Cad é,* Wicky?"

Mitchell ignored her and continued walking to where Mina lay.

"Mina, *cad a shamhlaigh tú aréir?*" Mitchell asked.

"*Shamhlaigh mé go raibh* Theresa *ag braiding mo chuid gruaige. Cén fáth?*" Mina replied.

"*Céard atá ag dul ar aghaidh?*" Theresa demanded again.

"*Tá an radharc caillte aici...,*" he said, a hint of anger in his voice as he cut the cloth ropes from the stretcher. It dropped several inches to the ground with a thud.

Mitchell grasped Theresa by her waist and pulled her down from the saddle. She winced from the pain in her knee as she impacted the ground.

Taking the reins from Hilary, he mounted the horse in anger.

"Wick! *Céard atá á dhéanamh agat?*" Theresa demanded.

"Tóg an cosán as a dtagann ceann thuaidh an tsráidbhaile! Ná trasnaigh isteach sna harbingers! Fan glan uathu! An dtuigeann tú?"

Theresa nodded without a word.

Mitchell's eyes softened slightly as he caressed her cheek. *"Beidh sé thart faoin am a thiocfaidh tú."* With that, the horse bolted away into the thick cover of black orchids. The strange flowers opened a narrow path before him and just as quickly closed off the path as he charged through them and down the hillside.

"Bloody Nora. What the 'ell just 'appened?" Katie exclaimed.

Theresa turned to Mina. "He asked you what you dreamed last night, and you said I was braiding your hair. Is that the truth, Mina?"

Mina nodded. "It's the truth! I wouldn't lie to you!"

"Nothing else?"

The girl shook her head.

"Everyone grab a corner of the stretcher. We best get a move on. Something is very wrong in the village."

"Thomas?" Melody asked fearfully.

Theresa rubbed her lips together as their eyes met but didn't answer.

They slowly descended the hill, following the harbingers to the north but not crossing into them.

The journey down the slope toward the village was slow going for the women and children.

Melody felt a bit of anger toward Mitchell for his rough handling of Mina and Theresa before his hasty departure, but she held her tongue as she still didn't know all the facts surrounding what had transpired in recent days. She also didn't know this man and chose to give him the benefit of the doubt.

She held her own grief close to her heart, choosing not to burden Theresa with the bad news of losing her job at the hospital and barely escaping the destruction of their house at the hands of the Nazis. She needed to share these burdens, but now was not the time. For now, her duty was to help her ailing friends to the village and see this nightmare through to the end.

36 Chapter Thirty Six

The Sheriff's Return

M ITCHELL SLOWED HIS pace as he entered the village. Smoke wafted toward him, as his home now seemed almost like a ghost town. There was no one to be seen… anywhere. He dismounted his horse.

As he walked down the main street, the Big House came into view. It had been burned to the ground. Smoke and flying embers filled the air as the wooden building smouldered. He paused for a moment at the bodies of his three best men lying facedown in the street. He gathered a rifle from one of the men's hands and checked its chamber. He cocked it in anger. Closing his eyes, he grieved the men at his feet.

Mitchell headed directly to Chloe's house as her front door was ajar. He entered to the sound of weeping. Moiré knelt at Chloe's bed as the old woman lay still. Mitchell's heart sank.

Moiré rocked forward and back with tears streaming down her face, gently dabbing a cool cloth to the old woman's brow. She was reciting the same words over and over: "I love you, Mum. It'll be okay. I love you, Mum. It'll be okay."

"Moiré, where is he?" he softly asked.

"I love you, Mum. It'll be okay. I love you, Mum. It'll be okay."

"Moiré!" Mitchell insisted. "Where is he?"

She pointed toward the stable, still speaking, still rocking, without missing a beat. "I love you, Mum. It'll be okay. I love you, Mum. It'll be okay. I love you, Mum. It'll be okay. I love you, Mum. It'll be okay."

Mitchell closed his eyes. After a long moment, he scrubbed his goatee with his fingers; he would have to mourn later.

He could still hear Moiré chanting as he approached the stable. Mitchell's senses were the sharpest they had ever been. He saw and heard everything around him with utter clarity. He could have easily swatted a fly or gnat into oblivion without even turning his head. He felt no pain from his injuries, just sheer determination and fury.

As he rounded the corner, his worst fear was realised. Thomas, looking viler than ever, stood holding Yavin in his arms—Mitchell's knife to his throat. Thomas's entire body shook, and his ashen face twitched.

Mitchell continued his angry march toward Thomas, not slowing his pace in the slightest.

"Here's how it's going to be!" Thomas began, his voice quivering.

Mitchell ignored him, looking his son directly in the eyes. "Boy! What do you do if you want a washboard stomach?"

Thomas, taken aback at Mitchell's anger, stammered for a moment. "Here's... here is how it's going to be. The boy for Theresa!"

Yavin hung limply in the man's arms, his face unsure of what his father was trying to convey to him. Then his eyes grew wide.

"Raise them high and keep them straight!" the boy cried out, lifting both his legs up, nearly toppling Thomas over backwards.

In a flash, Mitchell raised, aimed, and fired his rifle at Thomas's groin, all in a single motion.

The impact instantly put Thomas on the ground.

Yavin, dusting himself off frantically, ran to his father, grasping him around the waist.

As the remaining townsfolk approached, Mitchell stared down at Thomas, who lay face-first in the street. With his boot, he rolled him over.

Thomas looked up at him. "I… I'll be seeing you again. And next time, you'll give her to me. The banshee too. I'll end them… both…" The final breath leaving his body had a whisper of laughter to it.

"He's dead," Yavin said under his breath.

"Yes, boy, he is."

"No. You don't understand. He's dead."

Mitchell looked at Yavin, sharing an odd glance.

"When he was holding me, he was dead. His body is cold. The smell… I've been around bodies before. I… I could see and hear the flies milling about that hole in his head."

Mitchell stooped down and felt Thomas's neck. He stood suddenly, jumping back several steps, with a look of horror on his face. He wiped his hand on his trousers.

"Got bless it!" He looked into Yavin's eyes. "Let's keep this to ourselves, okay?" Mitchell said quietly, noticing a maggot crawling on Yavin's shirt. He silently flicked it off. "Son, go have a wash. Your hair too—a good wash. Toss those clothes you're wearing into the fire first. Okay?"

Yavin nodded with fear-laced eyes.

Mitchell turned to the others. "Put his body in the Big House. We'll let the fire he started take him to where he belongs."

Chapter Thirty Seven

Chloe's Passing

T HERESA STOOD AS close to the fire as she possibly could without being consumed in it herself. Thomas lay atop one of the collapsed and smouldering roof supports that now lay on the ground. His body was wrapped in death cloth, a treated and heavily perfumed muslin that helped mask the stench of his rotting and now-burning body. She wished she could see his face one last time, just to watch the flesh burn away from his skull.

She knew this was a slap in the face of her moral values but didn't care. The pain and pandemonium he had brought was only rivalled by those who waged war against her country. He was evil, pure evil, and Theresa hated herself at that moment for having been foolish enough to allow someone like Thomas and the destruction he brought into her life.

How could any of these good people ever forgive her? How could she ever forgive herself?

She turned and walked away, determined to never think upon Thomas again. As she approached Chloe's home, Thomas's body rolled off the support beam into the ash.

In Theresa's absence and Melody having taken to Chloe's bedside, Hilary took charge of the little troop, sending Katie off to help the villagers and Mina to bed while she attempted to console the inconsolable Moiré.

Mitchell and Theresa eventually found their way to the kitchen table and shared several pipefuls of tobacco and mugs of mead, keen for word on the old woman. Mitchell held Theresa's hand and seemed to be probing the contents of her palm using a strange tool.

"What do you call this?" he asked.

"Tweezers," she replied with a grimace as Mitchell extracted a sizable splinter of wood from her hand.

"I'm glad your friend brought her medicine-woman kit. This could have been lodged in your hand for years, maybe centuries. Festering! Pints of green pus, oozing and squirting out all over everything!" he quipped with a smile and saucer-sized eyes.

"Stop it!" She laughed and slapped his shoulder.

They sat in silence until Theresa spoke again.

"How can you stand to look at me, Wicky? After all the trouble I've brought you."

Mitchell shook his head. "The trouble wasn't you; it was him. If anyone is to blame, it's me. I should have put him down when I had the chance. I sensed wrongness in him. Darkness. And for what it's worth, I find you very pleasing to look at." His face turned red.

Theresa grasped his arm, squeezing it tight, and shook her head. "It's not your fault."

"Nor was it yours."

Silence again filled the room. Then Theresa continued. "I never got to ask you. How do you know so much about the Hidden Child and the otherworld? Are you from there?"

He shook his head with a smile. "I was born here, in this world, but my parents were from Hirtha. They came here as *Caomhnóirí Geata*— Guardians of the Gateway. We were all supposed to return before the portal was closed permanently, but something happened—we don't know what—and we were all stranded. After seeing the ship in that cavern and the way it was stuck in the wall, I suspect that is the reason."

Melody emerged from the bedroom after what seemed like hours, looking exhausted and grim.

"Theresa," Melody said softly, "Chloe would like to see you."

Theresa knew that look. Her eyes quickly filled with tears.

"What did that bastard do to—"

"It wasn't him. It wasn't him. It's just her time. She's *very* old. She's been keeping her illness to herself for some time."

Melody embraced Theresa as her tears began to flow. Mitchell dropped his head and closed his eyes. He knew what the tears meant.

Melody cut their embrace short. "Theresa... seconds. Only seconds left. Go."

Theresa entered the dark room. A single candle on the nightstand illuminated the old woman in her bed.

"I like her," a voice said from the near darkness.

"Pardon?" Theresa replied, wiping the tears from her face.

"Melody. I like her."

Theresa sat down next to the dying woman. "Me too," she said, trying to sound cheerful.

"I hear the elf is safe. That's good news."

"Yes. It was close, but she's going to be fine."

"Did you tell her?"

"Tell her... Who? What?" Theresa stammered.

"The elf, Mina. Did you tell her you love her?"

"Yes. Yes, I did!"

"It made a difference, didn't it?"

"For both of us, Chloe. It changed everything."

"I'm so glad." Chloe became silent for a long moment.

"Chloe?"

"I'm still here. I need to tell you something... something I forgot to tell you before."

Theresa gently caressed the old woman's face. "What's that?"

"Time… time works a little differently in the otherworld than here. It passes much more slowly. Your father may still be alive, Treena. There is still time to take the elf home to save our peoples and perhaps… perhaps to see your father again."

Theresa sat stunned at this revelation.

"Mina… Mina isn't the Hidden Child anymore," Theresa said. "She's no longer the Unloved Sacrifice. She is *very* loved now."

Another long moment of silence filled the room before Chloe responded, her voice now very weak. "She may… still be able to save our people. It's in her blood, Treena… salvation… in her…"

Chloe never finished. Theresa gently cradled the old woman's head as she pressed her wet face to it. She wept silently as the candle next to the bed went out, plunging the room into darkness.

38 Chapter Thirty Eight

Solitude

THERESA SPENT THE next several days in solitude, much of the time at Chloe's grave. She scarcely had any thoughts, feeling empty and silent within. Mina would join her from time to time, and they would walk together in silence, hand in hand, mother and daughter.

Melody, knowing Theresa well, let her mourn in her own way. She busied herself treating those injured during Thomas's rampage of the village. Four people had died, including the three he had shot and five others had been injured, mostly from burns, trying to extinguish the fires he had set. Melody did her best to comfort Moiré though the communication gap between them made that difficult. Still, the child quickly bonded to her.

The men began the monumental task of rebuilding the Big House. It would have to be completed before winter as it also served as storage for the crops and grains they depended on for their very survival.

Many of the women, including Hilary and Katie, took over the tasks of working the fields. Seed still needed to be sown, and Hilary found that she was a natural at tossing seed from the burlap shoulder satchel. Katie did not enjoy the task of weeding the fields but found great comfort in the little jam sessions she had become part of with her new musician friends, including Moiré, which they would enjoy together after the day's chores were done.

Both girls had begun to pick up bits and pieces of the strange language but still felt unsure of their place in this odd community. Hilary and Katie also felt concern over Theresa, who was isolating herself from everyone but Mina, but Melody reassured them she would be fine and to exercise patience.

On the fifth morning, Melody joined Theresa as she stood in silence at Chloe's grave.

"Hi. How's your knee today?"

"Oh fine. It's fine. I suppose you want to talk about going home, don't you?" Theresa stared out toward the Black Forest.

"Not really."

"Well, I'm not going back there."

Melody smiled. "Neither am I."

Theresa's eyes met Melody's. "You're not?"

Melody smiled again, shaking her head. "You are looking at the village's new doctor. By the way, does this village have a name?"

"I'm sure it does," Theresa said with a crooked smile and a shrug.

Melody lifted an old silver necklace with a fire agate stone in the middle from her neck and displayed it with a smile. "Medicine woman. Chloe gave it to me."

"Really?"

"Really."

"She also offered us her home with Moiré before she passed. Fact is, we don't have a home to go back to anyway."

"What happened?" Theresa realised she hadn't asked what Melody had gone through in the past few months.

"Nazis flattened it to the ground. Oh… I was sacked from the hospital last month too. Long story."

"Oh, Mel, I'm so sorry."

"The ceramic chicken survived though, as did Mr Pims! He's living with Old Lady Cabot now," Melody said with a smile.

"I'm very glad to hear that."

Theresa gazed at Chloe's grave. "Mel, I'm going to take Mina home."

"I know."

"You… you're okay with that?"

"I'll be waiting here for you both to come back. I have patients to look after—and a baby to deliver in a few weeks."

"A baby?" Theresa said with raised eyebrows.

Melody nodded. "A woman named Gwen. I guess they have babies in this weird place too!" They both laughed. "Learning this language is going to be a challenge though."

"You need to understand something," Theresa said solemnly.

"That Mina is your daughter? I understand and totally accept that as long as I get to be Auntie Mel."

Theresa smiled as she lowered her eyes to the ground. "Well, I'm glad to hear that, but that's not what I was going to say."

"What then?"

"Chloe told me that time works differently in the otherworld. It runs slower. We might be gone a very long time. At least it will seem that way to you."

"I know. Chloe told me too. She also told me that your father might still be alive."

"You could come too."

Melody smiled. "I understand that you have to do this for you and for Mina. I must stay and help these people. I hope you understand *that.*"

"I do," Theresa said with a smile.

"When do you plan to go?"

"In the morning. I've already talked to Mitchell about it. He's going to escort us through to the other side."

"Well," Melody said with a deep sigh, "I think we should spend some time together before you go. I want to hear everything. I want to hear all about your uncle, what you have been through, what this world you're going to is like, and most of all, how do I ask for a proper cup of tea in this place? No one speaks a word of English here!"

"*Bealtaine mé cupán tae,*" Theresa responded.

"Is that pig Latin?" Melody retorted with a smile.

39 Chapter Thirty Nine

The Final Meeting

T HE EVENING BROUGHT a meeting of the travelling troop and its newest member, Mitchell. Theresa shared her intent to return with Mina to the otherworld, pausing occasionally to translate the conversation to Mitchell.

Katie stared intently at Theresa, hanging on her every word, whereas Hilary kept her head down, fumbling with a loose bit of yarn on her jumper.

"When do we leave?" Katie demanded a split second after Theresa finished.

"Katie, as I said, it's just me and Mina. Melody's not even going. We need you to stay here and help rebuild before winter. *This* is our home now, and I plan to return as soon as possible to be with all of you. We are a family now," she said with a nod to Hilary, who smiled at her words.

"And Mina? What about Mina? Is she coming back?"

Mina, who had been silent to this point, finally spoke. "I'm planning on it, Katie. I'm planning to come back. I just have to do this, don't you know."

"Why? After all we've been frew! Why? You have a mum now. You have a home and family who love you. You don't need to do this."

Theresa shook her head in frustration. She had just spent nearly half an hour trying to explain the reasons. Katie either wasn't listening or simply chose to ignore her words.

"Katie," Melody broke in, "do you know much about fish?"

"Fish? Tha's not random at all. You want to talk fishing at a time like this?" She snorted.

Theresa leaned forward, pointing her finger directly at Katie. "Button it."

Katie quickly pulled her face as far back into her head as she could, her lips and chin all but disappearing completely.

Melody continued, "The salmon is a unique fish. When they reach a certain point in their life, they must swim all the way back upstream to where they were spawned or die trying."

"Mina's not a…" Katie stopped, blinking several times as she realised just how true the analogy was. Mina was mer. She had to go home… or die trying. "I'm going wif you!" Katie stated flatly. She sat back in her chair, arms folded.

"No, Katie. You have a home here and friends. What about your music?"

"Not one minute ago, you said we are family. Family sticks togevah. We don't go our separate ways or we're not a family. You cannae have it both ways! We *are* family. I'm going."

Theresa puckered her lips to one side of her face.

"You might as well give your blessing, Theresa. You know I'll just follow."

Theresa closed her eyes and nodded silently. She knew Katie well enough to know she would indeed follow them—unless of course she tied her to a tree, something she had no intention of doing.

Theresa shared the *Reader's Digest* version of the conversation with Mitchell, who looked none too pleased.

Katie, feeling victorious, folded her arms and turned to the silent Hilary. "You comin', Hils?"

After a long moment, Hilary spoke. "No. I've had quite enough adventure, thank you. I can be more help here."

"Seriously? Shut up!" Katie said in disbelief.

"Seriously. But I will see you to the doorway—or tree—whatever it is. I'll say my proper goodbyes there."

"Me too!" Melody added. "We'll all see you off properly!"

Theresa smiled. "It's settled then. We leave in the morning."

"Question, if I may," Katie asked with a raised finger. "Why don't we just take the boat? And why are these two portals so close togevah? Seems like poor planning by the portal commissioners, if you ask me."

"Umm…" Theresa's face contorted as she looked about the room for an answer. She couldn't find one.

Chapter forty

Pegasus

"THERESA?" MITCHELL SAID. "May I?"

Theresa nodded gratefully.

Mitchell ushered them outside and directed their attention to the sky. He looked about the stars, then pointed to a particular constellation. Theresa readied herself to translate.

"Katie, do you see that group of stars? It's called Pegasus as it looks a bit like a flying horse if you connect the dots. Do you see it?"

"I'm actually rather learned regarding astronomy," Katie replied after Theresa's translation—strangely, without her accent. "The ones surrounding it are Water Bearer, Andromeda, Cassiopeia, and Jupiter is the bright planet below and to the left. Ancient mariners used and still use the stars to navigate by, even today. Many of the names are from ancient Greek gods."

Theresa stared at her for a moment in disbelief.

"She said yes," Theresa replied to Mitchell, her eyes still on this strange Katie before her.

"Now imagine that Pegasus is wrapped around the earth, each point representing a portal. Some are closer together and some farther apart. Some will transport you quickly to the other world, but others, like the *Cirtolthiel,* are farther away and take much longer to arrive. The tree is small and direct, but only one person can travel at a time. The *Cirtolthiel* can carry an army and large weapons but takes much longer to reach its destination and must cross perilous waters to do so. They also exit at different times and different places. Does that make sense?"

Theresa translated Mitchell's words.

"Quantum physics 101. Interdimensional conduits and time dilation possibly preceding the passing through or near to a black hole. It never occurred to me that this could happen here on earth between two parallel universes, particularly without a black hole acting as a catalyst and creating a wormhole between the two. But what opens the conduit and makes it stable? That's the question. It would have to be something native to both worlds. A peculiar element... in a stone perhaps or a person or both. John Wheeler wrote in 1915, 'Space-time tells matter how to move; matter tells space-time how to curve.' Very Einstein-ish stuff. Right then. Fanks!" Katie suddenly picked up her accent again.

"She said yes," Theresa replied in a flat tone to Mitchell.

41 Chapter Forty One

Separation

THE MORNING BROUGHT heavy rain and wind. Lightning and thunder slashed across the sky like a sharp knife slicing open a burlap bag filled with seed and spilling its contents onto the ground at a frantic rate. The low-lying areas quickly filled with water that spread outward, flooding the roads and pathways.

Mitchell was soaked to the bone, his boots covered in mud as he carried the last of the supplies to the stable. They would be loaded onto the prax for the journey to the other world. As he walked by the remains of the Big House, something caught his eye.

About twenty feet from the building lay a pile of cloth. He set the supplies on a tuft of grass and slowly walked toward it. He stared at it, feeling a cold chill on his neck, then picked it up. It was Tom's death cloth.

"Got bless it," he muttered. Mitchell hurried over to the spot in the building wherein Tom's body had been placed. With a stick, he sifted through the ashes. Nothing. No clothing. No teeth. No bones. Nothing.

Mitchell assembled his men, instructing them to gather their weapons and take positions around the village. He hurried to Chloe's house and entered without knocking. His face was stern and his eyes focused. He scrubbed his goatee, which was rapidly becoming a beard, before he spoke.

"We need to get going. Now."

"Are you that eager to be rid of me, Wicky?" Theresa said with a wink and smile.

Mitchell grasped her hand, looking longingly into her eyes. "I don't want you to ever leave, Treena. I think you know that. But Thomas's remains are gone. I found his death cloth, and he's no longer occupying it. He's the Daemose. No doubt about it anymore."

"Oh my God…"

"I need to get you to safety. Someplace he can never hurt you again. After I see you through, I'm going to destroy the portal so he can't get to you or Mina. Meet me at the stable straightaway. Protecting you and Mina is more important to me than being with you."

The rain had slowed to a drizzle as Theresa, Melody, and the girls approached the stable. Mitchell stood waiting with two men with rifles at his left side. On his right was the fully loaded prax. Angst filled Mitchell's eyes.

Melody's eyes grew wide at the sight of the strange beast. She thought she had seen everything in this village. She was wrong. Its long, wiry mane and bizarre face seemed rather menacing, but there was a gentleness in its tiny eyes. A strange and rather unpleasant odour filled Melody's nostrils. She pinched her nose and began breathing through her mouth.

"This is Carl and Sean. They are going to accompany us to the doorway. You should say your goodbyes now. Time to go," Mitchell said.

"We had an argument. They're all seeing us off at the portal," Theresa replied apologetically.

"We don't have time for this. He's out there… somewhere."

"I know, Wicky, but I may never see them again. It's decided."

"Got bless it," he mumbled to himself with a sigh. "Right then. I've given you a week's supplies. That should be more than enough, given the supplies at the other *Wait*. After that, I would suggest heading south, toward Perth. There is a small village just north of it that will help you."

"Does this village have a name?" Theresa asked.

"Um… probably. You'll have to check the map. You have a map in the leather fold on the prax. Don't lose it."

Mina stroked the head of the beast, pressing her cheek against his face. The prax began purring.

"He won't fit through the door. He's too tall," Mina said, still caressing the beast's face.

"No, love, he won't. You'll all have to carry what you can once we get there." Mitchell replied.

"He's a good boy," Mina said softly. "His name is Mátamelcan."

Theresa and Mitchell smiled.

"Henceforth," Mitchell proclaimed, "this prax shall be known as Mátamelcan."

The heavy rain soon returned as did the gale-force winds.

The trees offered some relief, but it wasn't long before they were all soaked to the bone. Mina was quite cheerful despite the dreadful weather. She told Melody all about her home, the two moons, the oceans, the lands and its peoples, going into great detail about Mr Turly and their friendship. Melody listened intently, often asking clarifying questions. When Mina tired from hiking the rugged terrain, Mitchell gave her a piggyback ride until she was rested enough to continue. Theresa smiled as she watched the bond between them grow.

It was late afternoon when they reached the narrow path. It led to the hilltop where the old tree stood. Despite the chilly rain, they were relieved to have seen no signs of the Daemose.

Below the sloping ridge lay briars, brambles, and deadwood. The rainwater poured off the edge, creating a waterfall effect. The sticky squidge was now as slippery as ice.

"Everyone hold hands! Like a chain link! Hold them tight," Mitchell called out, "lest you be washed away!"

Theresa quickly relayed Mitchell's words to the others in English. No sooner had she finished speaking when Mina slipped sideways and promptly landed on her bum in the mud, her legs dangling over the edge of the ravine. Katie seized Mina's hand, but the narrow pathway beneath her gave way. Katie tumbled face forward down the steep incline, nearly taking Mina with her.

"Katie!" Mina screamed. Theresa and Melody grabbed Mina and Hilary, shoving them up the steep, rocky hillside as they all watched in horror.

Mitchell dropped the prax reins and rushed toward the spot where Katie had toppled over the cliff with Carl close behind him.

A five-foot section in the path was now missing. He summoned all his strength and leapt across the expanse. As the heel of his right foot reached the other side, more of the ground gave way. He landed belly first in the mud, both legs dangling off the edge of the pathway. He winced in pain, having landed on his still-sore ribs.

As the ledge beneath him crumbled, Mitchell slithered belly first to where the ground seemed more stable. Carl followed but didn't quite make the jump to the other side. He cried out for help, clinging to a rock that was quickly giving way.

Mitchell grasped his arm and pulled him to safer ground as the rock tumbled into the ravine. Carl gave him a nod of gratitude. Mitchell peered over the edge of the cliff to find Katie hanging upside down, only held in place by her foot, which was lodged in the loop of a protruding tree root.

Another section of the path gave way behind them, and everyone watched in horror as Mátamelcan toppled over the edge into what was now a rushing river.

"Mátamelcan!" Mina cried out in a mournful voice as she struggled to regain her footing. Theresa quickly pulled the girl into her arms.

"Stay still!" Mitchell commanded the upside-down Katie, who flailed about wildly, screaming and swearing. The loop in the roots holding her foot in place cracked at her weight and movement.

"Stop struggling, child!" he commanded again.

Mitchell turned to Sean. "Get them up the hill—on all fours! Crawl up the hill. Use the trees and plants as grasps and footholds! We'll get Katie!"

Mitchell motioned to Carl, who hooked the front of his boots around a small tree still planted firmly into the ground. As Mitchell prostrated himself over the edge of the cliff toward Katie, Carl grasped Mitchell's trouser belt. Mud and water rushed over them. Mitchell stretched out his hands toward the terrified girl below.

"Katie! Reach up! Katie!" he screamed desperately as the mud filled his eyes and nostrils. "Katie… Katie please," he pleaded.

After what seemed like minutes, he suddenly felt a hand grasp his, and he squeezed it tightly. He began pulling the girl toward him. Soon she had her arms around his neck, and he and Carl strained with all their might against the water and mud rushing down upon them. Mitchell set her securely on the ground before attempting to clear his eyes of the stinging mud. She grasped his neck and sobbed. After a moment, Mitchell motioned to Carl with his head and eyes, and they began the ascent toward the others, Katie still clinging to Mitchell's neck.

The rain and wind had slowed to a breezy mist when Mitchell, Carl, and Katie reached the hilltop. The others greeted them with tears of relief but great concern.

"Where's Sean?" Mitchell asked.

"We don't know," Theresa confessed. "He was with us when we were climbing. Then he wasn't. We called out for him, but—"

"Got bless it. Keep a weather eye all about! We're not alone!"

Katie's eyes grew wide at the surreal, charred surroundings before her.

"It's called the Devil's Playground because of all the lightning strikes here," Mina said. "Something about magnets."

"Magnetism?" Theresa asked.

"The rocks are a blackened-rust colour. Could be iron or possibly something peculiar with the magnetic field up here, being so close to the interdimensional conduit. Either or both could account for the multiple lightning strikes and hence the nickname of this area," Katie stopped short, realising what she was saying, "What's 'appening to me?" she asked fearfully to no one in particular.

"Katie, do you know what a fugue is?" Theresa asked.

"You're starting to remember," Mina whispered into Katie's ear.

"Remember what?" Katie demanded fearfully.

Suddenly several bolts of lightning struck the ground about them, accompanied by an ear-splitting snapping. It raised the hair on their necks and arms and made their ears ring. A horrible sound resembling a man shrieking in agony from a lightning strike could also be heard in the near distance.

"Time to go!" Mitchell announced.

The shredded shell of a tree stood at the edge of a steep cliff. Its single remaining root bore deep into the rock, splitting the rock in two. Mina lifted the key from her neck as Mitchell readied his axe over the root. Carl stood by his side, standing watch, both men precariously close to the cliff's edge.

Flies began gathering all about them. Hilary and Melody tried slapping them away. Theresa turned the key, its inset stone glowing slightly as she pushed the door inward.

The small door creaked open, displacing ancient spider- and cobwebs. It was pitch-black inside. The old, musty smell entombed within met their nostrils.

"Katie! You're first. Go!" Theresa said as she hurried Katie through the doorway.

"Mina! Go! Go, go, go!"

Theresa crawled, legs first, into the opening. She looked back at Mitchell with longing in her eyes. She could feel her body being pulled into the vortex.

"Wicky, I can't lose you again."

"I love you, Treena. Always have," he said, stopping suddenly as the smell of rotting flesh intruded into his nostrils.

To Theresa's horror, Carl was suddenly wrenched off the cliff to the rocky ground far below. Mitchell quickly took aim at the remaining tree root with his axe as hundreds of flies began buzzing about him.

"Go!" he screamed as his axe fell.

The last thing Theresa saw was the corpse of Thomas rising up behind Mitchell from the cliff wall. Part of his flesh had burned away, revealing the skull around his eye and temple.

"Wicky!" she wailed as the dry water wrenched her into the darkness.

Theresa felt herself being pulled down a pathway at breakneck speed. In the blackness, she felt her head collide with something very hard. Searing pain enveloped her—and then darkness.

Theresa opened her eyes and lay still without a single thought. She grasped a handful of earth and watched the soft grey silt filter through her fingers. She stared and slowly wriggled them, moving them close to her face. She closed and opened her eyes several times, hoping her vision would clear. She felt something trickling down her forehead. She wiped the liquid from her brow and studied it, blinking numerous times whilst trying to focus her eyes in the strange, dim light. She was quite certain it was blood though it appeared grey. The world was colourless. Everything before her was either a muddy black or brownish grey and seemed very grainy, like a photograph taken in faint light.

She lifted her head slightly and stared at the skeleton of the old tree lying on its side some ten feet away. Two ghostly figures appeared beside her and grasped her by the arms.

Theresa struggled against the figures, finding it difficult to move and breathe. The air about her seemed thick and unyielding. She found herself gasping for air. The only sound was a strange, rhythmic pounding in her head. All else was silent. She laboured to sit up. The ground below her would seem firm for a moment, then suddenly give way, becoming soft silt. It reminded her of a giant crème brûlée. After three attempts, Theresa managed a sitting position with help from the ghostly figures.

She looked at the figures on either side of her. After a moment, she recognised Katie though her facial features were distorted and seemed washed out. The figures knelt next to her. Katie had a blank expression on her face as she stared at the ground.

"Are you all right?" Theresa said, stopping suddenly and placing both her hands on her ears. "I… I can't hear. I can't hear my own…"

Katie grasped Theresa by the hand. "Can you hear now?"

"I can hear you—wait. I can hear myself. Sounds… weird… hollow and tinny."

"Sound waves," Katie replied. "They don't travel right 'ere. Nor light waves. We can only hear if we are in direct contact. I was becoming very concerned. It's been hours. I didn't know if you were going to make it."

"Hours? I was right behind you. Seconds behind Mina."

Katie nodded. "Probably the time displacement. Mina was nearly an hour behind me."

"Mina? Where's Mina?" Theresa said frantically.

"I'm here, Mum. Right here," Mina said, holding Theresa's other hand.

"I saw Thomas! Are the others okay?"

Katie shook her head slightly. "Don't know. Hopefully, whatever power was keeping him… animated was severed with the tree root. Mitchell did cut the root, didn't he?"

"Yes. His axe was falling when I came through. I'm sure he did. I can't get it out of my head," Theresa said with a quiver in her voice.

"Get what, Mum?" Mina said.

"Thomas. He was a corpse. A bloated, burned, rotting corpse that was moving. I can't unsee it."

Both girls held Theresa close as she wept.

"Hopefully, Thomas dropped when the connection was broken," Katie reiterated, trying to comfort Theresa. "I'm shoh the others are safe."

Theresa rose, staggering slightly as she stood, her head throbbing angrily. Katie and Mina remained unmoved, their eyes fixed on the ground. With the girls no longer obscuring her view, Theresa's heart sank.

The once beautiful world that she and Mina were from was no more. Total desolation surrounded them. The entire forest was burning, with a thick layer of smoke and ash covering it as far as she could see. There was not a single standing tree in sight except for a few charred stumps that stood scattered like blackened tombstones in an old graveyard. The *Wait* had been burned to the ground as well. They would find no sanctuary there.

Mina reached up and took Theresa's hand. "We're too late."

Chapter forty Two

Something Evil This Way Comes

T HERESA AND THE girls, struggling to breathe in the soupy air,
walked the perimeter of the hilltop, surveying the damage and
chaos below. To their horror, a battle was raging all about them. An
army with bows and arrows, swords, shields, and spears was decimating
a smaller group of what looked like medieval peasants who were only
armed with clubs and rusted, poorly crafted swords—in silence and
frozen in time. They looked like waxwork figures carefully placed in
combat positions at a museum.

"My God," Theresa said. "What is happening here?"

"It's the crossing. We'll be okay in a few days," Mina replied.

"Crossing?"

"That's what I call it. Dunno the real name. It happens when you
cross over through the portal. It'll catch us up."

"Catch us up to what?" Katie asked sceptically, her face contorting
in disbelief.

"This. Time is different in both worlds. It goes slower here.
Everything is moving, just very slowly. It'll take some time for us to
adjust," Mina said.

"Fascinating," Katie replied. "So this is a side effect from interdimensional travel. We are actually witnessing *and* experiencing time displacement of two distinct and separate time pockets—at the same time. This is supposed to be impossible. It's like looking at a photograph of yourself and someone else many years past and then being able to interact with the people in that photograph years later. No, wait. That's a terrible analogy. Scrap that. Even so, that explains the light spectrum shelling out one colour of light at a time. We are out of sync with this world. It's supposed to be impossible, but here we are, living proof of it, and yet we can to some degree interact with this otherworld by being in actual, physical contact with it, at least for a brief moment. What's the time factor for total synchronisation?"

"A week or two," Mina replied.

Theresa knelt and placed her hand on what looked like a torch that had been dropped in battle. As her fingers met it, it sprang to life, burning her hand with wild red, yellow, and blue flames. As she recoiled from the fire, the torch and its flickering flames froze in place again, becoming colourless and benign.

She held her fingers as she studied the now-motionless torch.

"I think you hit the nail on the head, Katie." Theresa grasped both girls' hands. "We best get a move on before they catch us up—or we slow down to their speed, yeah?" Theresa said.

Katie nodded. "We'll be in some very deep sh—"

Suddenly a fly buzzed by Theresa's face and then by Mina.

"What the...?" Theresa said, swatting at it. All eyes moved toward the portal exit. Flies, one by one, were exiting the doorway.

"Oh no. No. No. No," Theresa whispered.

They watched the flies entering an open wound in a sword-wielding soldier just above the ridge of the trees. As Theresa crept toward the man, she guessed that this was probably the leader of the army as he wore the armour of a high-ranking officer.

Theresa crept ever closer, unable to hear the screaming girls protest behind her.

She looked deep into the man's eyes, his wild gaze focused on the enemy before him. Suddenly the eyes, one at a time, moving in a juddered motion, fixed upon her.

"Hell… hello, luvah. Miss me? Give us a kiss!" the raspy, distorted, almost metallic-sounding voice finally said before freezing in place again.

"Run!" Theresa cried out. "For God's sake! Run!"

To be continued…

Acknowledgements

Very special thanks to those who helped make this book possible:

Mumm's the Word Editorial Services:

Anita Mumm, You are amazing! Thank you for your incredible developmental edits and for teaching me the craft of writing. I have a long way to go, but your efforts were life changing and I am grateful for you and your patience with me.

Victory Editing:

Anne, thanks to you and your team for your awesome line-editing work and prep for publication. I couldn't have done this without you! Thank you so very much! I am so grateful to you all.

Creative Paramita Book Cover Artist:

Paramita Bhattacharjee, your cover design, brought to life the story and its spirit. Your work as always, is amazing! Thank you!

I also wish to thank several musicians, as their music was a direct influence and inspiration to the story:

Loreena McKennitt:

Her studio version of Prospero's Speech was the inspiration for the siren's song. I visualise Lir rising from the water, singing this song to seduce her prey.

The studio version of Huron 'Beltane' Fire Dance, was the inspiration for the song that Theresa was so desperately trying to remember-the song that awakened the spirit of the trees and harbingers. She finally remembers it at the celebration and the power of the chant saves the entire village from Thomas.

Bear McCreary:

The Irish tune, The Dance, from Battlestar Galactica, inspired the dance scene in the big house. I love that happy ditty.

Trevor Jones:

The Kiss, from The Last of the Mohicans, is a powerful and moving instrumental tune which inspired Moiré's playing, The Song of Loss.

Thank you all,
MK Shevlin

Printed in Great Britain
by Amazon